STORIES FOR SPECIAL DAYS
IN THE CHURCH SCHOOL

MARGARET W. EGGLESTON

HIS FIRST OFFENCE

From a painting in The Tate Gallery, London, by Lady Stanley.

STORIES FOR SPECIAL DAYS IN THE CHURCH SCHOOL

BY

MARGARET W. EGGLESTON

Author of "Around the Camp Fire with the Older Boys,"
"Fireside Stories for Girls in Their Teens," "The
Use of the Story in Religious Education," etc.

WILDSIDE PRESS

PREFACE

Today there is a growing realization of the fact that the first half hour of the Church School is as vital, if not more vital, than the last half hour. Teachers are insisting that the superintendent's worship hour shall create an atmosphere which shall prepare the way for their lessons. Superintendents everywhere are crying for help in preparing for this half hour. And it is well for our pupils that such is the case.

Our libraries are full of stories that MIGHT be used; stories that in the hands of a trained story-teller could easily be made very much worth while in conveying the religious message. But if not adapted to the thought of the day, they often fail in their mission.

Especially is this true of stories for special days. There are many, many flag stories but few that will be easily adapted for use. There are wonderful mother stories in our libraries but they are hidden away in books of biography, history and art. So the superintendent who has little time and little training finds it more and more difficult to satisfy the growing number of teachers who are seeing the vision of the worship hour of the school.

I have chosen these stories from among many, many others which are in my files because they have proven their worth in my own work in the Church

School. I have told them to large groups and to small groups, and have seen them carry their message. Many of them are planned especially for the Intermediate and Senior Departments, because I know how very difficult it is to find material adapted to the work in those departments. I have chosen stories that my own young people have loved to tell, hoping that they may also be told by the young people in the churches. One of the very best ways to create a desire to be a teacher is to train a boy or girl to be a good story-teller. It is a field to which we have given little attention and yet which is just waiting to be worked.

Many of the stories have been taken from the lives of my friends and acquaintances; some were told to me on a recent trip to the Near East; the story of Ahni was told to me by a missionary who is now dead. I believe it to be a bit of her own work. If it has ever been printed, I shall be glad to acknowledge the author; but I have never seen it nor heard another tell it. The Living Christ, The Knight of the Bath, and the Knight of the Cross were published in The Church School and are re-published with their permission.

I have suggested how the stories might be used. But others may easily be fitted into the special day by adaptation. For instance, at a recent Mothers' and Daughters' Banquet, girls told five of the stories in this book as Mother Stories. Plan the theme of the service—loyalty, sacrifice, courage, enlistment, etc., and then tell the story to fit the theme of the day.

To be effective, a story needs to be electrified by the personality of the story-teller. This can hardly

A SUGGESTED LIST

New Years
    A New Year's Story

Memorial Day
    Ask U. S.

Good Friday
    For Love's Sake

Easter
    At Easter Time
    A Little Child Shall Lead Them

Missionary Sunday
    Mary Matthews' Missionary Package

Rally Day
    The Life Saver
    Two Steps Forward

Thanksgiving
    Ahni

Christmas
    On the Hills of Bethlehem

Young People's Day
    Her Roadway—Its Mission
    The First Offense
    Its Mission

Mother's Day
    For Mother
    The Legend of the Wings

Enlistment for Service Day
    Marjory's Gift
    The Life Saver

CONTENTS

CONTENTS

STORIES FOR SPECIAL DAYS
IN THE CHURCH SCHOOL

STORIES
FOR SPECIAL DAYS IN
THE CHURCH SCHOOL

A NEW YEAR'S STORY

WE are very cold when our thermometer stands at zero, but in the land called Labrador it is often more than thirty degrees below. We could scarcely keep warm in our steam heated houses, but they must live in old huts where there is little of comfort or cheer. We grumble if we must wait on the corner for the street car, but they must drive for hours across the snow and ice in their open sleds drawn by teams of dogs.

Yet into that drear and cheerless country a hero chose to go. From north to south he drove his team of eight dogs during the winter; steered his little boat in the summer, ministering to the bodies of those people, leaving health and happiness behind him. So big was his parish that only once in several months could he visit a station to care for those who were sick.

Wilfred T. Grenfell, one of the great men of the world, had been far back inland to see a sick woman. She had needed medicines which he did not have, so back again he had driven to get them. But when he came to the station, he found there a message asking him to come quickly in the opposite direction to see a man who was dangerously ill.

The men of the town had all gone for the whaling season. What could he do? There was no one to send, yet one of the two would die if help was not sent to them. He could not go in opposite directions, much as he would have liked to have been able to do so.

Finally he turned his team in the direction of a little village not far away. Here lived an eleven-year-old boy who had learned to be a "Jesus Boy." And as he drove on the doctor thought,

"I hate to ask him to go for it is such a long, hard trip. It is all a new road for him and he is such a little fellow. But he has a dog and he is trustworthy. So I am going to ask him to go."

When he came to the home of the boy, Dr. Grenfell explained his difficulty and then said,

"Are you strong enough and brave enough to go for me? Will you be my helper and try to save the life of the woman?"

Now the boys of the Labrador love this man who has done so much for their land and their homes. There is little they can do for him but they are glad to be asked to help. For a moment the boy thought it all over—the bitter cold, the long, long, journey, the unknown way, the dangers which he might find on the way——

Then he just bravely answered his friend,

"Doctor, I no know the way; I no know the place; I no know how I can ever get there with my one dog. But I can try. I will go."

And he did. He carried the medicine, guided

only by his compass and the stars, across the miles and miles of trackless ice and snow to the sick woman. He saved the life of a mother of the Labrador. He proved that he was really a "Jesus Boy."

ASK U. S.

HER eyes were dark and full of enthusiasm. Her skin was burned almost black by the sun of the desert. Her face showed more than the usual intelligence of the Armenian race. She was Araxie, a girl of sixteen who had recently been a pupil in an American School in the mountains of Asia Minor.

For four years she had studied there and had proven herself to be one of their very best. Then the news of the taking over of the mission station by the enemy had closed the school and all the girls had been sent back to their homes in the villages. To Araxie this was a sad message. She loved the school, she loved the teachers, and she was so eager to learn that every day lost seemed so hard.

When the day came for them all to go, Araxie went to the teacher in charge and said,

"You remember the old flag which was put away when the new one came from America. Couldn't I have that flag to take home with me. I love your flag and I wish I could have it."

"And what would you do with it?" said the teacher.

"I would put it away and only take it out to look at it sometimes when I was lonely for our school," said Araxie.

So she was given the flag, and lovingly she carried it to her little home in the hills. In that home there was only a grandmother for the father had been killed while fighting to protect their village. So Araxie went back to help to make the living for the two of them. Provisions were very high. There was little food to be had and often the two of them were hungry. But they loved each other and did their best.

Then one terrible day there came the word that they were to be massacred. Most of the population of the little village fled for their lives. But the grandmother was ill and they could not flee. The face of the girl grew white with terror as she heard the yells of the soldiers as they came near to the village. What could she do? How could she save them? Only too well she knew that probably she would be taken as a wife by one of the soldiers. Should she take the life of herself and her grandmother and so save them from a worse fate?

But God had forbidden one to take life. God! Ah! He could help to save them. Running up to her little room, she knelt by the table and prayed,

"Help us, O God! Hide us from the soldiers!"

As she rose from her knees, she saw her school box in the corner. Then with a cry of joy she ran to it and pulled forth the old United States flag which she had so often drawn to the top of the pole of the mission station. Running downstairs she called,

"Grandmother, grandmother. I have the flag—my flag from the school. Perhaps that can help us."

Quickly she fastened it across the doorway of the home. Five minutes passed. She heard people hurrying down the street but no one entered the home. Then a half hour was gone and still they were safe.

A band of soldiers halted in front of the door, talked about the flag and then went up the street. Soon more soldiers came. It was plain to be seen that they did not understand the meaning of the flag. Finally the captain of the band came to the door.

"What does this flag mean?" he said. "Why should you, Armenians, be protected by that flag?"

Araxie's heart beat very fast as she looked him directly in the face.

"It means, sir," she said in good English words, "that grandmother and I are under the protection of that flag."

His face grew dark and angry. He could not understand her. Yet he knew that she was speaking in the language used by the country that owned that flag.

"I can speak to you in your own language, also," said the girl. And she repeated her statement. "See! This will prove it to you." And turning to the corner of the flag, she showed him some words, written in the English language.

"This says, 'If you are in need, ask U. S.'"

The Turk looked at the writing and then at the girl. She was very beautiful and he wanted her for his own. He wanted to reach out and steal her away from the rest. But his orders had been strictly,

"Touch nothing that belongs to the United States government."

For a moment he hesitated. Then he turned to his men and said,

"Pass on. We will see about these two women later on."

Next day another officer came, and again Araxie read to them the words written in the corner of the flag and signed by a well known American. He also, dared not touch her while that flag hung in front of her door.

After a time the enemy left the village. Few friends were left alive to help each other and Araxie knew that, sooner or later, she must flee for her life. But where? How?

As the days went by, the grandmother grew worse and at last, worn out by the worry and danger, she left Araxie alone in that little Armenian village. Then the girl knew that she must go quickly before the enemy should come back.

Getting together what she could, she started across the hills, traveling by night. Sometimes she lay for days in hiding until the bands of soldiers should pass her. Three times she was nearly caught. Her face grew thin and careworn as the days went by. But finally she came to the coast, one hundred miles from her home. Here she knew that she could find foreign vessels. Perhaps she could also find some Americans.

But she had no money? What could she say to them? Would they take her away from danger? How could she find a way to speak to them? Again she turned to her precious flag. Wrapping it tenderly in a package, she waited until the next vessel from Greece came into the port. Taking a few of the coins that she was so carefully hoarding as they grew less and less in her bag, she went out in one of the little boats to the steamer.

"Is there an American on board the steamer? If so I have a package for him," she said to the captain.

"There are two," said the captain, "Wait in the cabin and I will send them to you."

When the two men, with wonder on their faces, came to the cabin, they found a girl waiting for them. On her lap was spread an old American flag. Looking earnestly into their faces, she said quietly,

"Will you please read this note that is written in the corner of my flag?"

And the men read, "If you are in need, ask U. S."

"I am in need, sirs. This dear old flag which flew over my mission school has saved my life from worse than death. I have a jewel here which I think will pay my passage to America, if you will take it. May I go in your care to the land which owns this flag which I love? I ask no favor of you except the protection of your name until I get to America. I will be of no trouble to you," said the girl.

The captain, the men, and several women on board the boat held a conference while Araxie waited. How eagerly she listened! What could she do if they said, "No."

Finally the elder of the two men, he whose hair was white as snow and whose face was so kind and true, came back to the girl and said,

"We know little of the value of the jewel. But we do know that when one asks protection of that flag, it ought never to be refused. We will take you to America and trust you to repay the debt."

Six years have passed by since that day and today the flag hangs on the walls of the room of a social-service worker in one of our Eastern cities. Her debt has long since been paid, but not in money. It has been paid, as her friends asked that it be paid, in helping to make the foreigners in our cities love and reverence the flag.

Often when the day is done, the girls will gather about her in her room and she will tell them the story of the day when the teacher in the school, just in fun, wrote in the corner of the flag which had floated over the school so long,

"If you are in need, ask us."

"Two little periods were all that I added," she says to the girls. "But those two little periods made the word 'Us' read 'U.S.' and that stands for the best country in the world. It made the torn, old flag the only friend that I had in the whole world who could help and save me. I am an American now so it is really 'MY' flag. See! I have put the writing at the bottom so that you can read it. It may say to you,

'If you are in need, ask us here in the mission.' Or you may read it as I did back in the home in Armenia when the Turk was ready to take me away,

'If you are in need, ask U.S.'

Either of us are ready to help the girls and boys of the world."

FOR LOVE'S SAKE

ON the back of the camel there were piles of bedding, baskets of dishes, and bags of grain and fruit; on the backs of the donkeys were bundles of clothing, a little stove, two chairs and many other strange things. On the backs of the parents and children were huge, odd-shaped bundles.

They stood before the door of their little home in Cilicia with fear in their hearts and tears in their eyes waiting for the orders to go. They were Armenians, ordered to leave their home with only a few hours' notice because they believed in God and were true to the name, "Christian."

The orders had been, "Leave your homes as they are for you will be back in a few months and we will keep them for you." But the Armenians knew better, so they had taken all that they could possibly carry, hoping that their fate would not be as hard as that of their neighbors who had been exiled some months before.

Gathering the little family about him, the father prayed to God to keep them together and to guard them from harm. Then slowly he said,

"I hope that I can stay with you but God only knows. All other men have been killed or worked to death. If they take you from me, remember how I have loved you and remember that God still loves you. I am hoping that somehow Fareedy here may still be the 'Chosen of God,' for we promised her

26

to God ten years ago. We must all be brave and
loving for hard days are ahead."

Scarcely had he risen to his feet when a band of
Turkish soldiers came rushing down the street, ordered him to drop his weapons and march in front
of them; and the father joined the long line of men
who were never heard from again.

Then the long line of exiles started for SOME-
WHERE. The sun was very hot and many died
by the way; there was no water and others lost their
minds and were left by the way. Some were
trampled by the horses of their captors. Little children who had to be carried were often thrown by
the Turks into the rivers and so the friends from
the village grew less and less. But still the little
family were together. There was slight danger of
the boys being taken from her for they were strong
and well. But Fareedy caused her mother many a
heartache. She knew that some day a Turk would
see how beautiful she was and steal her away.

So she cut off her pretty hair. She dressed her
as a boy. She kept her very close to her side as
they hunted the fields for food. Sometimes they
were out on the desert; again they were in the hills.
Sometimes they stayed several months at a time in
a place; again they wandered wearily on and on.
Often it seemed to the mother that she must drop
by the way. But for the sake of the children she
kept on.

Then one of the boys grew very sick. She tried
to carry him but he was very heavy and she lagged
behind. The children tried to help but they
stumbled and fell. And then—a Turk threw him
aside and forced the rest to move on. Fareedy's

black eyes blazed as she looked at the man, but quickly she drew back for he was reaching for her.

More months passed and the second brother went to be a shepherd in a home near by, so now there was only the mother and Fareedy. And every day as she grew there was more and more danger.

One day, when they were again on the march, they were ordered to do some work for a company of Arabs and as they worked, the mother heard one say,

"That is no boy. See how good-looking she is. I am going to have her for my own." And with spear in hand and evil look in his eyes, he took Fareedy by the arm. The mother fought like a tiger. She begged that they take her instead. She offered to give her life for the child. But only blows, and curses, and laughs were her answer. With his great whip he drove her back until, wounded and bleeding, she fell to the ground and saw them lift Fareedy to the horse and ride away.

Oh the days that followed! Her body was full of pain and her mind was in torture. What would they do to her child? She had been consecrated to God. Would He not save her? Where had they taken her? Somehow she would find her. But how?

The weeks passed by. Every time they passed exiles she asked if they had seen her little one. But thousands of children had been stolen. How could they know which one belonged to her? Almost hope had gone when one day, in a band coming from the north, she found a woman from her own village.

As soon as she saw the mother, she said,

"Have you lost Fareedy? I am sure that I saw her tending sheep in a field many days to the north of here. There were three girls and I am sure she was one."

That night when all was still, a figure of a woman might have been seen creeping along the ground away from the exile camp. She had started for that place many days to the north. A little bundle of things under her arm were all that were left of the old home. Inside the bundle was some hard, black bread which was all that was between herself and starvation. Would she find springs on the way?

Would some one be kind to her and give her to eat? She did not know. She must find her child some way. As best she could, the woman had told her the way, though the mother knew she could not go by day, or travel along the beaten path. But on she went.

The days that followed were full of pain and suffering. Sometimes she lay for hours, too weak to move. Sometimes she had only grass to eat. But nearer and nearer she came to the place where the child had been seen. She began to inquire whenever she dared.

"Has a new shepherd girl come into the fields? Have you seen one with hair cut short like a boy's?"

One day her heart leaped with joy for a boy said to her,

"Did she have a little limp when she walked? Yes I saw her once on the farther hill."

"And is she still there?" asked the mother eagerly.

"No, none of those girls are there. They were all bought by a big Turk and he said he was going to take them to Damascus where he lived. I was in the field when he came to take them from the sheep," answered the boy.

"And was he kind-looking?" said the disappointed mother. "Oh, my Fareedy, shall I ever find you?"

But the boy didn't answer. He only grunted and went on with his sheep.

Damascus! Oh! how far away it was! Could she ever get there? Once the father had been there, and he had told her of the walled houses in the big city. How could she find her if she did get there? But on she went. Sometimes she stopped to work for a day or two to get bread to eat. Her body was so thin and so tired. Life was a long, hard road.

Then she came to Damascus, after days of traveling across the hot, hot desert. Here she knew that she could find friends and help. So she rested for a time and then began her search. Only in one way would she know Fareedy. Her body would be covered with a long dress; her face would be covered with a heavy veil; but nothing could hide her limp. So she sat on the street corners selling things out of a basket and watching for a woman with a limp. She spent hours in the bazaars watching the buyers. If Fareedy were in Damascus, she was sure that some day she would find her.

And she did. Long before the child reached her, the mother saw her. Waiting until she came very close, the mother first asked her to buy, and then she said quietly, "Fareedy, is it you?"

There was a little cry of joy as the girl recognized her mother, but she dared not talk to her. She pressed her mother's hand very hard as she laid a piece of money in it and said,

"I will come when I can for a minute. Be here at eleven."

When the mother had learned where she was and what she was doing in the harem of a Turk where his many, many wives lived, she went to a mission school in the city and told them her story. She gave to them a jewel which she had carried all these long, weary months since she left home, and she made them promise that if the girl came to them, they would keep her safely and train her to be a worker for God.

"Long ago we promised her to God and I must keep my promise," said the mother. "I do not know how she can come but if she does, keep her and love her for me. I give her to you and the church."

The next day when Fareedy came to the corner, her mother drew her quickly into a little room near by.

"Quickly," she said, "Take off your clothing and give it to me. Put on mine and take my basket. Then go quickly to this street and number and you will be safe. Hurry child!"

"But mother, you can not go to the harem. They would kill you if they found that I had deceived them. My master is hard and cruel. Look at the great scars where he has beaten me. He will kill you. No, I will not let you take my place."

Bending low over her, the sad-faced mother said,

"Fareedy, long ago I gave you to God. He has helped me to find you. I am now old and feeble. I have a disease which must kill me soon. If I live, I must be poor and lonely. You can live and be well and strong. You can be cared for and be happy. You can be a 'Chosen of God.' If you love me, hurry! I am glad to free you because I love you better than life."

A few minutes later both were ready. There was a long and tender farewell. Then an old bent lady with a basket on her arm went down the street toward the mission school. When she had been gone long enough to reach there, a Mohammedan woman in a long, black dress, a long, heavy veil, and who limped as she walked, went up the street toward the harem. She looked at the house and a deep sigh escaped her. But on her face there was a wonderful light. She had saved Fareedy and given her again to God. She had shown her mother-love.

Then the door opened and she went inside.

No one knows what happened within. Perhaps she is still there, working for the Turk. Perhaps she is at rest.

Many, many miles over the hills and the desert, in a school for girls, Fareedy is working and studying. Her face is very sweet; her heart is very tender; her character is very lovable. She is "Chosen of God." She will be a teacher.

Often as the sun sinks in the west, she looks toward the old home, thinking of father and his courage; of the little brothers and of the brave mother. Then she says to herself as she turns her mother's ring round and round on her finger,

"Dear Mother. With her own life she ransomed me. I must repay her with a life of work for God."

AT EASTER TIME

GERTRUDE MARLOW sat before the fireplace in her pretty home looking at a letter which the postman had brought to her. Twice she laid it in her lap, after reading it, with a face that was scornful and angry.

"Lilies for the Easter service at the church!" Indeed she didn't care to send them. Why should she when she had no use for the church or religion now! The farther she could keep away from the church the better she liked it. Then, little by little, she went back in thought over the last two years.

Mother had loved Easter lilies and, always, they had gone together to the church to fill the font in memory of the little brother who had died. She could remember many, many times when they had done so. But now mother was dead and for a year the home had been so lonely. Since the last Easter the friend to whom she was to have been married had been killed and so, now, life seemed to have nothing in it for her. She had an empty home, plenty of money and nothing to do.

At first when her loved ones had gone, she had been dazed; then full of questions. Why should these things come to her? She had done no wrong. God was unjust, unfair. There was no love in her religion. Who knew that there even was a God?

So, as the days went by, she had just shut God out of her life until her heart became a vast empty tomb with a great stone of contempt rolled before the door of the tomb. No wonder her lip curled when she read the letter. They wanted her to send lilies as mother had done for so many years. Perhaps mother liked to remember that God had taken her little boy, but she certainly thought differently.

Hastily she tore the letter in pieces and threw them on the fire. Then she sat down at her desk, wrote a note saying that she did not care to send the lilies and then called for her car, in order that she might go to the florists and order flowers to wear in the evening. The only way which she had found in which to forget the past was to go, and go, and go.

She was seated, deep in thought, as they rolled down the street when suddenly there was a scream, then a jolt, and then the car came to a sudden stop. The people rushed to the street and as she stepped from the car, they lifted a child of twelve from beneath the wheels of the car. Her head was covered with long, yellow curls and as Gertrude brushed them aside, she saw a dear, little face that was white as the driven snow.

Tenderly they placed her on the seat of the car and started for the hospital. There was no scratch to be seen but she lay, pale as death, on the cushions.

The moments seemed hours, and the hours seemed days, as she waited for the doctor to come from the operating room. Then he said quietly, "She has been hit in the spine. She will live, perhaps, but she will probably never walk again. Her hip is badly broken."

It was two.days before they admitted Gertrude to the room where the child lay so white and still.

The room was the best that the hospital afforded. On the stand was the great bunch of flowers that she had sent. Yet as Gertrude looked at little Mary, there was only one sentence that burned itself into her brain,

"What can I do? Oh! what can I do to help her?"

Sitting down by the bed, she talked with the child and found that she was an orphan whose mother had died but a few months before. She had been sent on an errand by the matron of the orphanage and was crossing the street when the car came around the corner. When Gertrude asked her if she was in pain, she answered,

"Yes, I have many bad pains and the weight that hangs from my foot is so heavy. Sometimes it seems as if I must take it off. But it is so nice to have such a beautiful room and such a good nurse that I try to be good to please her."

When the time came for visitors to leave, Gertrude bent over the little white bed and said,

"Mary, I can give you any comfort that you need. I can come to read to you. I can bring you anything you may want to eat. You may have all the flowers that you want. Will you tell me any time when there is anything that you would like? I want to do something, dear. I want to do many things for you while you have to lie here. Please tell me."

And Mary answered simply,

"I can't think of a thing that I could possibly want—but if there is anything, I will tell you."

As Gertrude Marlowe sat before her fireplace as

the evening shadows fell, her mind was full of the
bravery and sweetness of the child in the hospital,
and as she thought of the things which she could
do to make her happy, a ray of light penetrated the
tomb within her, and she felt a glow of warmth
within.

Not many days later, when she came to the sick
room, she found Mary with feverish cheeks and a
restless body. Back and forth she tossed, in spite
of all the nurse could do.

"I am so glad you have come," said Mary. "I
have been waiting for you. Can you sing?"

"Indeed I can," said Gertrude. "Would you
like to have me sing for you?"

"Mother used to say that it helped a lot," said
Mary. "My leg is so heavy and tired and I want
to see my mother. Please sing, and I will close my
eyes and make believe she is singing to me."

So Mary closed her eyes and Gertrude sang.
First there was a little spring song and then a lul-
laby. As she sang Gertrude saw one big tear after
another go rolling down the face of the little suf-
ferer. As the second song was ended she said
plaintively,

"Mother used to say hymns helped her most.
Please try one. I like the new one we were learn-
ing for Easter—'There is a Green Hill Far Away.'
Can you sing that?"

Almost the singer said, "No." She felt the bit-
terness rising within her at the very name of the
hymn. She and mother had sung that so often together. But on the cheek of the little girl was the
tear and she did want to help. So, falteringly, she

began the dear old hymn. Twice she sang it very slowly,

> Oh dearly, dearly has He loved,
> And we must love Him, too,
> And trust in His redeeming love,
> And try His work to do.

But when the song was ended, the little one was asleep. With a smile of gratitude from the nurse, Gertrude crept out of the room and lo! another dark corner of her heart was lighter as she said over and over to herself on the way home,

"Mother says hymns help most when the pain is there."

It was the Saturday before Palm Sunday when she found the pastor of the little church sitting by Mary's bed, holding her hand and bringing smiles to her face.

"Mr. Baner knew mother," said Mary, "and we have been having such a good visit about her. I have been telling him how you sang to me when I felt so badly and now I have thought of another thing that I would like so much to have you do. You know I was to sing all alone at the church to-morrow and they have no one to take my place. Those boys and girls at the mission church never hear any one sing as sweetly as you do. Will you please go to the church tomorrow and sing in my place as the boys and girls come up the aisle? Mr. Baner says it would be wonderful to have you there and then I shouldn't feel so badly about having to miss all the service. You can sing it to me when you come again and that will be as good as being there, maybe. Will you go?"

Oh! the struggle as the little girl had been talking! Surely she must say no. But Mary had said, "Then I shouldn't mind so much about having to miss the service." What could she do? She had no excuse to offer. She had promised to help in any way that she could.

So Palm Sunday morning found her standing at the altar of the little church and singing for Mary's sake,

> Hosanna, praised be the Lord.
> Bless Him who cometh to bring us salvation.

And as she sang, the stone of contempt was rolled away and again she loved the beautiful song. The prayer of the minister helped and in the simple sermon she found again the love and goodness of God.

Very early on Easter morning, Gertrude Marlowe's car stopped before her mother's church and left lilies for the font in memory of her mother. Then she stopped and left some at Mary's little church to remind the boys and girls of the brave, little friend in the hospital. Then she drove to the hospital. Down through the wards she went and wherever there was no lily, she left one as Mary's gift.

When again she came to the lower hall, a friend was waiting for her. A moment of soft music on the piano, and then there floated through the halls and into the sick rooms a wonderful song. The voice of the singer was full of love and sympathy, and her face was full of happiness as she sang,

> Christ, the Lord, is risen today, Alleluia.
> Our triumphant holy day, Alleluia.

But in the room of the little sick girl there were two glad voices singing a little later,

> Oh dearly, dearly has He loved,
> And we must love Him too;
> And trust in His redeeming love,
> And try His works to do.

So the stone was rolled away from the door of the tomb and within there was light and joy and beauty. For she had risen with Christ to a higher life.

"AND A LITTLE CHILD SHALL LEAD THEM."

WHEN Mary Katherine Dale came home from her gymnasium class on Thursday afternoon, she found a dainty little note waiting for her. It was from Mrs. Brice, she knew, and she thought it might be an invitation to a class party. Instead, she read these words,

"DEAR MARY,
"I have just received a note from Violet telling me that her mother is very ill and so she cannot attend to the decorations for the church on Saturday. We want it to be very lovely for Easter Sunday, you know. You are the only one of my girls who is free at that time, so I am writing to ask if it will be convenient for you to do the work for me. You are free to decorate it just as you please with the lilies and palms which will be sent there. Some of the younger boys and girls will be there to help you. Thanking you for your help which is always so willingly given, I am,
"Sincerely,
"ALICE BRICE."

After the letter had been read, there was silence for a moment and then the girl said to her mother,
"Evidently Mrs. Brice has forgotten that I am not in her class in the Bible School any more. Why I haven't been there for six months, at least, and yet she is asking me to do the things just as if I were

40

still there. I suppose I shall have to do it to please her, but I certainly don't want to spend a lot of time there on Saturday."

"But why not?" asked the mother. "You used to love to go there and help. I have let you do as you wished about going to church, Mary, hoping that in time you would see that you wanted to go because of the strength that came from the work and the worship. But I really think you ought to be helping there still."

"But, mother," said the girl, "why should I go? I don't believe all those things that Mrs. Brice believes. Since I began to go to college, I have beliefs of my own that please me better than theirs. Then, too, they are always asking me to join the church. I don't want to join so I just stay away. Why should I join a church?"

Mrs. Dale did not answer but on her face was a look of pain. Why was Mary so different from the rest of her girls? Was college going to take from her the best things in her life? She seemed to care so little for sacred things nowadays. And, deep in her heart, Mrs. Dale was glad that they had once more asked Mary to help.

Saturday afternoon was bright and sunny and the girls had telephoned Mary to go for a hike with them, so there was a cloud over her face as she entered the pretty little church about two in the afternoon. In a corner of the room were many palms, and below the altar steps were some tall Easter lilies. But no one was there to help, so Mary began to find the things needed for use. First she started for the rear of the church to find the standards for the palms.

But as she went through the hall she heard a moan—and then another. Mary turned pale and started for the door to run away, but she stopped. Perhaps John, the janitor who had always been so kind to her, had been hurt and needed help. She searched through the hallway but he was nowhere to be seen. Then she went into the chapel but he was not there. So she turned again to the church and as she entered the door, she heard a big heart-breaking sob, and then a tiny voice said,

"Mother! I want my mother!"

Mary hurried to the place from which the cry seemed to come and there, almost hidden by the lilies, she found a little, dirty, ragged boy. His yellow head was covered with curls, but they were matted close to his head. His face was streaked and dirty. His blouse was torn and faded. His feet were bare and cold.

Bending low over the little fellow, Mary said gently,

"What is it, sonny? Have you lost your mother? Come and let me help you find her."

But the answer was only a sharp cry and a drawing away from her. His little body shook with sobs and Mary could see that he was very, very tired. So, forgetting the pretty dress which she had been so anxious not to soil, she picked him up in her arms and carried him to one of the pews. Then she held him close until his sobs grew less, and less, and quiet came.

"Where is she? Where is she?" he suddenly asked.

"Why I don't know," answered the girl. "Do you know?"

"No, I don't know at all. They brought her here yesterday in a big box. They told me she was asleep. Won't she wake up pretty soon and come home? I want my mother. Please find her and wake her up," cried the boy.

Then Mary knew. This was one of the little boys whose mother had been killed in an automobile accident. What ever could she do? Surely she could not help him. To whom could she take him? But a little hand was stealing into hers and a little voice said,

"Can't you tell me where she is? The lady that lives next door said she would never come back. But she will, won't she? If she won't come back, can't you take me where she is? Where is my mother?"

"Why—why—why mother has gone to live with Jesus, dear. Mother was very sick and if she had stayed here she would have had to be very, very sick for a long time. So she has gone to live with Jesus and he will make her well," said Mary.

"And who is Jesus?" said the boy, looking deep into her eyes.

Mary thought for a moment, and then tenderly lifted the boy in her arms and carried him across the hall to the pretty classroom of the Beginners' Department. There, sitting on the chair near the beautiful copy of "Christ and the Children," she tried to tell the story of the loving Jesus to the child. The big, blue eyes opened wider and wider.

"Then she will never be hungry again?" he asked.

"No, never," said the girl.

"And he will never beat her as father used to do?" asked the boy.

"No, Jesus is kind and gentle," she answered.

"And some day I can see her again and live with her there where He is?" asked the boy.

"Yes, if you try to be kind and good also," said Mary, holding him very closely.

"How do you know?" he suddenly asked.

Then, like a flash, Mary felt weak and helpless. That was one of the things about which she had been questioning. But now two eyes were looking straight into hers, waiting for her to tell him how she knew. For a moment she hesitated. Then she said quietly,

"I know because this good, kind man said so, and he never told things which were not so. I am very sure."

After a time the two went back into the church and he watched her arrange the palms and the lilies, all the time asking questions that made her think deeply. So the hour slipped by, and she was sorry when the work was done and it was time to try to find out where he lived. He knew the way and so the poor little home was soon found, and she hurried on to her own home, saying over and over to herself the question which he had asked her,

"How do you know? How do you know?"

All during the evening, the face and the need of the little child were before her and, little by little, she saw how much less she was able to help him because of the months away from the Church School. Now she felt again the happiness of helping. Now she knew that once more she wanted to be very sure that she loved the "good, kind man" of the picture.

Early on Easter morning Mary went to the room of her mother and told her the story of the little child. She told of her efforts to help him and of the lesson that it had taught her.

"I wish I were to join the church today with the rest of the girls," she said. "But it is too late now. But I want to go back to the class today and learn to be a real helper."

If you were to go into one of our large cities today, you would find at the head of a great hospital a sweet-faced woman who has given her life to helping God's little ones. Often she sits in her office in the evening and talks to a young doctor who calls her Aunt Katherine. To him she has been friend, and sister, and mother, since the day when she found him in the church. He is the little child who led her to a life of service.

MARY MATTHEW'S MISSIONARY
PACKAGE

THE class of girls was being dismissed from the mission school, and as they turned to leave the room the teacher said happily,

"Remember, girls, it is to be something that you love and yet want to give to some other little girl. I know now what I shall bring. But you never could guess what it is. Let's come early so that every girl can see what every other girl has brought."

"I shall give my new, red ribbon," said one.

"I think I shall bring, 'Polly of the Hospital Staff,' for I love that book best of all," said another. "But I shall miss it at bedtime."

"I shall give the pretty box of handkerchiefs which came to me at Christmas," said the third.

But Mary Matthews said nothing. What was there in her home that any little girl would want? She looked at her dirty dress, all streaked with lines where she had tried to clean it as the teacher had asked her to do. She thought of the torn books in her home. She hadn't even a handkerchief to bring, and she knew mother would not let her take it to the mission if she had one. No, she had nothing to give. She would stay at home on the following Sunday for she had nothing that another little girl would like.

And sure enough, every girl was there, except Mary, when the following Sunday came. They put their gifts into a big box, and then talked about the color, and the home, and the life of the little girls in the land to which they were going. But not one of the girls thought of the real reason why there were eight gifts instead of nine.

Now Mary had been thinking all of the week about that box into which the gifts were to be put. She knew just how it was to be trimmed, and just where it was to be put. So about ten minutes after the School had closed she crept up to the door of the mission and peeked in. There was no one there so she was quite safe. Then she went into the room where her class was held. Yes, there was the box with all the packages nicely tied and addressed. Quickly Mary reached under her dress and took out a very flat package; looked again to make sure that she had written correctly the address which the teacher had given to her the previous Sunday; dropped the package into the box and then ran out of the mission.

But as she hurried down the street, she wiped some big, big tears from her eyes as she said,

"It was the only one I had. It was dirty because I have looked at it so much, but I loved it and it was all that I had. Maybe she hasn't many clean things so she won't notice that it isn't very clean. I wish I had another."

Many, many months later, the little box stood in the hallway of a queer house made of grass in Africa and two missionaries were taking out the parcels, one by one. When they came to the flat, dirty little package, Mrs. King said,

"That has come from some little girl who didn't have much to give, I am sure. See, it is for Ndibi.

I had forgotten that I sent her name with the rest. I will take it to her this very afternoon."

So the package was taken to the home of a little cripple girl who for months and months had lain on her hard bed, hardly able to move in the least. Her face was drawn with pain, and her eyes were red with crying.

Ndibi took the little, dirty package and, never seeing the queer wrapping, she untied the string and looked within. Then she gave a cry of happiness.

"See," she said. "See the big, big lion and the queer little lamb! Here is an old leopard right by the lion. See the little girl! The old lion seems to like her and she isn't afraid. How could that be, Mrs. King? Over in America where this little girl lives, do the lions play with little girls instead of eating them as they do here? I have wanted a picture to put here by my bed for such a long, long time and now I can have one. What a good little girl she was to send it to me! Tell me about it, please."

So the missionary told her about the picture as best she could in a few minutes, placed it on the grass wall above her bed, and went away.

Several weeks later a man came to the church and said,

"We like that picture that Ndibi has. Wouldn't some one come down and tell us about it?" Then the missionary found the house full of men and women waiting to hear about the picture. And out of the number grew a class to study about God.

But one day the picture blew to the floor and when it was picked up, Ndibi saw that there was writing on the back. Again the missionary was sent for and she read these words to Ndibi,

"This is the only nice thing I had to send you. But this little girl always said to me, as teacher said she would,
'Don't be afraid if things are hard. God will take care of you.'
I shall miss having this little girl in my house but I hope she talks to you, too. Good-bye. Mary."

Then the little girl in the picture began to talk in that queer grass home in Africa. She talked to Ndibi and made her cry and fret less. She talked to Ndibi's brother and helped him to go to school after a time. She talked to the mother, and the father, and to the friends who came into the house.
Finally she talked so plainly to Ndibi that she consented to do what the mission doctor had wanted her to do for a long, long time. She took a hard journey in a cart to the coast where there was a mission hospital. There they cut away some of the diseased part and gave her a chance to be well and strong. When they had placed Ndibi on the table ready to operate and had put her to sleep, they felt something which she had been hiding under her night gown, close to her body. What could it be? The nurse slipped her hand inside and she drew out—what do you think?
She drew out a picture of a little girl standing very close to a lion, and a calf, and a leopard, and a dear little lamb.
The picture was very much more soiled than it had been when Mary Matthews had given it many

months before.   But it was not too much soiled for
one to read, written on the back of it,

"Don't be afraid when things are hard.   God
will take care of you."

Little Ndibi had believed it, and so she had taken
it with her when she went such a long, long way
away from home, to stay for many long weeks, and
to suffer pain.

Mary had thought, "No little girl would want
what I have to give"; but Ndibi thought, "What a
good, little girl she was to send the picture to help
me grow strong and well."

THE LIVING CHRIST

YEARS and years ago there lived in the city of Copenhagen in Denmark a young man whom all the world was to honor, Bertel Thorwaldsen. There in his humble home he learned to shape the clay, to cut the marble, and to make simple, beautiful statues.

After a time he felt that he must go and study under the great sculptors who were to be found in the countries south of Denmark, so he left home and friends to go to Italy, and for twenty-three years he lived and worked there.

But the call of the homeland was very strong, and when he heard that statues were to be made for the church which he loved, he left Italy and came back to his old home. The great blocks of marble were brought to him, and as the days went by they grew into wonderful statues, thirteen of them, statues of the Christ and His twelve disciples. When they were finished and placed in the Church of the Frauenkirche in Copenhagen, they seemed almost alive and ready to help in the beautiful services which were held there.

From far and near the people came to see them. All were beautiful, but it was the statue of the Christ which claimed most of the admiration. Pure and white the statue stood, showing the living Christ with His hands held out to all who came. Some stood long before it; some seemed to gather great

comfort and to go away from it cheered and helped;
and some knelt in prayer for forgiveness and
strength.

One day there came to the church a group of
people who had been searching Europe for the
great and beautiful. Church after church had been
visited; one museum after another had been studied
till finally they had come to the little country of
Denmark to see the greatest of the Thorwaldsen
statues. Down the long aisle they came, stopping
often to look at the face of the Christ. How gentle
He seemed! How loving His face! How tender
His whole attitude! So, as they gazed silently at
the statue, no one noticed the little old lady who
helped to keep the church clean, standing, also, at
the foot of the statue. No one thought that to her
the statue meant even more than it did to them.
She was only the person who brushed away the dust.

But that little old lady loved the beautiful Christ
and she wanted others to know Him as she knew
Him. So she watched them as they studied it.
Standing close to her was one of the young girls of
the party. Touching her dress, the little old lady
said, "When you stand there you cannot see how
beautiful the Christ is. You must not only look into
His face, but you must look into His eyes. And
that you can only do from your knees."

So the little old lady and the young girl knelt
together on the floor of the dimly-lighted church.
And they saw the wondrous beauty of the living
Christ.

THE LIFE SAVER

O N the wall just in front of the dresser was a
picture of a boy. He had a round, freckled
face, a splendid body but a defiant look. Below it
hung a medal for life-saving. And in front of the
picture and the medal stood a tall, fine-looking fellow of twenty-five, Arthur Sands. When he looked
into the face of the boy in the picture, his own face
lighted and a smile ran quickly across it.

"Homely as a bulldog," he said, "and just as
stubborn, too."

But when he looked beneath the picture at the
medal, the smile faded away and he said thoughtfully,

"What a hard fight that was! I nearly lost him.
But if he had gone down, I should have gone too.
We can both be glad that we won."

He was re-living a day earlier in the summer
when he had been the hero of the hour in a seaside
resort. A group of newsboys had been brought
there for the day and he had enjoyed watching
them have their fun in the water. Bob Bates had
attracted him from the first because he was so little
and so full of mischief. After several hours of fun,
there had come a cry from the water. An undertow
was carrying Bob out to sea. And Arthur Sands,
athlete and crack swimmer at college a few years
before, had gone after the boy.

It had been a long, hard fight. Both had lain for

more than an hour unconscious on the beach at the end of the fight for life. But both had lived. And then during the few days that followed, when the boy had been the guest of the hotel, they had become so well acquainted that the older man had become, "Uncle Art," and the boy had become "My Bob."

Then the boy had gone back to his work and the man had stayed to finish his holiday. This was his first Sunday back in the city and he had written to Bob that he would take him and some of his friends on a ride to the country, if they would meet him on a certain corner. "Enough to fill the five passenger car," he had said and he was wondering if they would be there to welcome him.

"How glad I shall be to see Bob again," he said to himself as he glanced at the picture. "It is strange how I love the little fellow. He wasn't always clean and his language is so disgusting. Yet I love to be with him. I wonder if I shall like his friends."

When the car stopped at the corner, Arthur Sands drew a long breath of surprise. On the corner waited Bob and six other boys. How could he take so many? But Bob's quick eye detected the question,

"I know I asked a lot of the fellers to come but ye see—well they will sit two deep all right Uncle Art. I just had to ask 'em for I wanted them to see you. I told them how you saved me up there in the water," and Bob snuggled close to his hero.

Well they piled into the car and away they went, far out where the country was very beautiful and where they could play as much as they liked. And

as they played the man watched them. How full of
energy they were! How their faces glowed as they
played! How well they followed the leading of
Bob!

Then he played with them and together they
came to know each other as only friends can do.
Finally they all sat together near the close of the
afternoon, eating some peanuts and preparing for
the trip home.

"And what do you fellows do usually on Sundays?" asked Uncle Art.

"I sleep most of the day." "I work at the beach."
"I stand on the corner with the fellows." "I shoot
crap most of the time" came the answers, quickly.

"Don't any of you go to church?" asked the man.

"Church?" said Bob. "They don't want us in no
church. Some of us went one night to that red
brick church. But we got put out. They don't like
our kind. No, we don't never go."

"But they do want you there. That is my church
where I go every Sunday morning. I know they
want you. I wish you would come again," said
Uncle Art. "Why not come some Sunday and sit
with me?"

"And what could we do if we went?" asked one
of the boys.

"Oh, sing, and read the Bible, and the minister
preaches very good sermons," said the man.

"Heh!" said the boy. "I thought you meant come
to Sunday School. I don't want to go to church.
Say, if we came to Sunday School, would you be our
teacher?"

"Oh, my!" said Bob, "I would come every Sunday if you would be our teacher. Will you?"

"Well, you see," said the man, "I don't go to Sunday School. I used to go when I was your age and I liked it too. I had such a good teacher and he and I are good friends today. You boys ought to go to Sunday School. I will ask the superintendent to find you a good teacher if you will come."

But the boys shook their heads. Some of the fellows had gone once and didn't like it. So Uncle Art said no more and soon they were back at the corner where he had found them, all happy over the wonderful time he had given them.

That night when he went to his room, he was thinking of them. He was thinking of the fact that they had been to his own church and then gone away again. Here were six boys who ought to be in the school but who had no desire to go. How could he help them? Ought he to say he would go to teach them?

But that would mean giving up his Sunday dinner at the golf club with his many friends. That would mean the preparation of a lesson every week. That would mean giving time during the week to them, if he did for them what his teacher had done for him. He was too busy to do that. And besides he had never taught: he surely would make a failure of that. He would talk it over with the superintendent and see if something couldn't be done to get them there.

Yet even as he settled it in his mind, his eye fell on the inscription of the medal:

"For his heroic efforts in saving the life of a boy."

Here was the chance to save the lives of seven boys—not one. He had not hesitated to offer his

life when Bob needed him in the water. Why
should he hesitate now? Was there not just as
much danger that these boys would lose in their
struggle for manhood. Three of them had no
homes. None of them had good homes. Who was
going to help them?

There was the little room at the church where he
had sat as a boy. It had been unused for some
time. It would make a great club room. Perhaps
he could keep them in off the streets at night if they
had some place to go.

But his own nights were spent at the City Club.
How could he give up his own pleasure for the sake
of six boys and Bob. Ah! but Bob! He loved the
little fellow. Could he see him grow up with no
chance? He had saved him from the water but
suppose now he grew up with temptations all about
him and no one to help. Might he not wish some
day that he had let him drown? Arthur Sands was
studying to be a lawyer and only too well he knew
about what boys *might* become.

He turned out the light and tried to sleep but he
saw the boys all about him. He saw them happy
and contented as they played with him in the country. Then he saw them going about the streets,
hunting for something to do. He saw hands reached
out all about them, seeking to drag them into the
nets of wrong.

The morning found him still undecided. He
wanted to help but he did not want to take the time
to do the work as he knew it should be done. He
believed in the Sunday School but he wanted others
to do the work.

Passing the church later in the week, he saw a

beautiful poster which had been placed there for Rally Day. It was a picture of the Christ with out-stretched hands calling to those who passed by,

"There is much to be done. I need your help."

How much was he helping? He went to church. He gave regularly. He belonged to several committees. How much was he really helping? When God needed help in winning him, his good old teacher had said,

"Here am I. Use me."

God was saying, "I need your help." The boys were saying, "We need your help." There was room for them and a welcome for them but only when they wished to come, would they do so. What could he do?

Finally he decided to make a test. He would give himself to the work for three months and test it out. He would say to the boys that for three months he would work with them, and play with them, and help them, if they cared to come. Then, by that time, another could be found who would take his place and he could be free again.

He knew where to find Bob on his corner calling out his papers. So he hurried to the place.

"Bob, my boy," he said, "up at our church is a little room in the tower that is just big enough for the bunch that came down to the country with me. How would you like to belong to a club that should meet there? We could meet on Sunday for an hour and study our lesson together and then we could meet another night and have some fun there all by ourselves. What say you?"

The boy's eyes sparkled as he looked up at the

man. His face seemed more freckled than ever as he turned it up toward his friend, and said,

"A lot of times this week the fellows have said that they wished you would teach us. We'll all come but say, get a big room for I have lots of friends who would like you. Uncle Art, I am awful proud to know you."

And he hurried down the street saying over and over, "A club of our own and Uncle Art to teach us. My! Ain't that great!"

Nearly ten years have passed since that day. That city boasts a great Newsboys' Club today and one of the directors of the club is Arthur Sands. He has in his office a picture of a little fellow with a round, freckled face. Near by he has a picture of seven boys who met with him in the tower room of that red brick church on that Rally Day ten years before and who formed the nucleus of the great Newsboys' Club.

Then he has many, many pictures of other boys whom he has known in these ten years which have passed. East and west and north and south they are scattered, but to them all he is Uncle Art—their best friend.

Not to every one does he show a little medal which is in a case on his desk. It used to tell of a boy saved from the water but now it speaks to him of many, many boys whom he has helped to save. And when he showed it to me and told me the story, he said earnestly,

"The happiest hours I have had in my life have been those spent in fighting for the life of a boy. I am so glad that God needed me to help."

TWO STEPS FORWARD

IT was Rally Sunday in the King's Street Sunday School and neither the pastor nor the superintendent were very sure just what was to happen. During the summer some of the young people of that school had attended a week of summer school and there they had learned many new things. Then they had called together some of the teachers of the school and told them of the new plans about which they had been talking. Finally they had gone to the pastor and asked to be allowed to plan the Rally Day service for the Young People's Department and see what they could do to help in the work.

Bob Kingston was to be the leader, and Bob was one of the biggest mischiefs in the school. How could he lead a service? Probably he would spoil it all. Mary Leeds was to sing. She had a good voice but she would be likely to refuse at the last moment. The superintendent was very sure that it would have been wiser to have had their "usual" Rally Day program.

But nine-thirty found a group of young people in their place and the service began. Bob stood tall and straight before them as he told them of the wonderful week which some of the young people had had. He told them of the work which the young people of the church had been asked to do. He said they had promised that King's Street would help and so they had come to ask for volunteers.

"When they want to create enthusiasm in the army, they sing," said Bob. "Let us sing, 'True-Hearted, Whole-hearted, Faithful and Loyal.' All who are ready to work, please sing." And the superintendent saw the group singing, with all their hearts, the inspiring song.

The lesson read was from the story of Joshua. He was to lead the children of Israel out into the new land and Moses was giving him his blessing.

"Only be strong and of good courage," read another boy, whose knees shook with fear. "The Lord thy God shall be with thee whithersoever thou goest."

Then Mary sang. The members of the school leaned forward in their seats. Who had thought she could sing like that? But Mary had caught a vision when she had heard some one at that summer school say,

"Sing your way into the hearts of boys and girls. Sing as if God were saying the words through you." So she sang as sweetly as she could,

> It may not be on the mountain-top,
>   Or over the bounding sea;
> It may not be on the battle front,
>   My Lord may have need of me.
> But if by a still small voice he calls,
>   To paths that I do not know;
> I'll answer, "Dear Lord, with my hand in thine,
>   I'll go where you want me to go.

Then Bob rose again and said,

"Out on our western front the soldiers were having trench fever. The doctors had done their level best but still it raged. Finally a serum was found that *might* stop it. But the serum had to be tried on healthy men. Five hundred men of New England were lined up before the officers.

"Men," he said, "I need sixty men who are not afraid to give their lives for the sake of others. I need sixty men who want to make the camp and the country safe. Many of you may die from the serum but by your death thousands will be saved. All who will volunteer step two paces forward when the order is given."

The officer turned about. The order was given. He heard a sound of feet but it seemed as if only a few had offered. Almost he feared to turn about. But when he did so, he found that every man had stepped forward—every man wanted to make the camp and the country safe by giving his own life.

"Boys," said Bob, "I want fifty fellows who will make this community a safer place for little children. I want to have better pictures in the moving-picture place down the street. I want a playground where the children can play. I want some boys to teach the little fellows. I want fifty girls who will help to teach the girls, who will help to make our socials better, who will help to make a higher standard for our work.

"During the summer, they asked us to invest our lives and we have begun this morning. We ask you to join us. As we sing, let us stand; let us think; let us ask God to show us how we can invest our lives."

A reverent song, an earnest prayer and then the little invitation,

"Those who will offer to use their lives to make our church better, our lives truer, and our community safer take two steps forward."

And the department moved forward as one.

Did they mean it? Did they do it? Indeed they did. The Sunday session grew in numbers and in worth. They gave of themselves in places where they were needed and God blessed their gift. The work went forward because "they had a mind to work." And all because a group of young people had caught the vision and then given it to their companions.

AHNI

BECAUSE Ahni was a little girl she was not welcome in her home in the far-off land of Korea. So, from the very first day that she came into that home to live, there were hard, hard things in her life. Often she was hungry; often she was beaten; always she was unhappy.

Of course her mother loved her, even though she couldn't do the things for her that she could have done had she been a little boy. So when her father was angry and tried to beat her she would run and hide somewhere near to her mother so that she might be safe from harm.

Ahni was only five years old when her mother died and then her father sold her as a slave. She had a sweet, little voice and so could earn money by singing on the street; but her father didn't want her so he just sold her to another man. Then Ahni was more unhappy than before. Her work was hard because she must hunt for wood, take care of the many babies in the home, and work in the rice fields. She had little to eat. Her bed was only some straw on the floor in the corner of the hut. She had no one to keep her clean and well. Her shoes were full of holes, and the cold of the winter crept inside and made her feet sore and lame. She had no mittens to keep her hands warm as she stood on the corners to sing her little songs to the people who passed by.

Finally, when Ahni was twelve years old, she

became sick and helpless. She could neither walk,
nor work with her hands. She suffered much with
pain, but she suffered more from the cruel words
and beatings of her master. At last he would have
her in the house no longer, so he took a stick and
drove her from the house. He pointed to a large
house on the hill—a mission hospital—saying,

"Go up there and if they cure you, come back and
work; but if they cannot make you well, never come
back to this house again."

Ahni had learned to mind, so she crawled along
the streets and up the steep hill to the hospital.
What would they say to her? Would they make
her well again?

But by the time that she reached the top of the
hill she was too tired to ask, so she lay in a little
heap on the door step, waiting for some one to come.

It was a kind-looking, young doctor who almost
walked on the little bundle of rags on the steps.
But when he saw the little girl who was dressed in
the rags, he picked her right up in his arms and carried her into the hospital. There she told them her
story.

First they gave her a bath in a big, white tub.
But Ahni had never had a bath like that and she
was afraid of the water; she was afraid that it
would hurt her sores; so she just screamed with fear.
But when she felt the soothing touch of the nurse
as she bathed her, she begged to stay in the warm,
sweet-smelling water.

Then she was taken to a white bed. Ahni had
never slept in a bed, and she could hardly believe
her good fortune when the nurse turned back the
white coverlet and placed her between the two

clean sheets. They rubbed the sore legs with medicine; they combed the tangled hair; they placed on
her a clean, pretty nightgown. Then the nurse,
with a heart full of pity for the little homeless girl,
bent over her, kissed her on the forehead, and said,

"Sleep now, little girl. We will care for you and
love you here, you may be sure."

But Ahni couldn't sleep. No one had kissed her
since mother had gone away and that was so long
ago that she could just remember it. No one had
loved her, and now this sweet-faced lady had said
that they would love her and care for her. Ahni
was so happy that it hurt.

As time went by, the nurses came to love her
dearly. She was so patient, so cheerful, so grateful
for all that they did for her. They did everything
in their power to make the wounds on her body
heal. But they had been there for such a long time;
they had been so cruelly neglected that they would
not heal, and so Ahni had to go to the operating
table three different times. And there they took off
both hands and one foot. Ahni was then more
than thirteen years old but she looked like a little
girl of ten as she lay in her wheel-chair, day after
day, in the sunshine.

Sometimes she seemed to be thinking very, very
hard. She had no home and no friends. How
could she ever walk with only one leg? How could
she ever learn to work with no hands at all? What
would become of her when the wounds were healed
and she had to leave the hospital? But most of the
time she was learning to sing the beautiful hymns
which the nurses sang to her; she was learning to

tell the stories of the Bible which the doctors told to her when they sat beside her in the sunshine.

One day, many weeks after her leg had been cut off, one of the nurses told Ahni that another nurse was going to America, and that she would see the little girls who had given the money for the bed in which Ahni had been lying for so many months. She would see the little girls whose pictures hung just above the bed, every one of whom Ahni had given a name.

"And could I send a message to those little girls?" asked Ahni.

"I am sure nurse would be glad to take it for you," was the answer.

So, a few minutes later, she went sliding along the floor of the hall until she came to the room of the nurse. She pounded with her little stubs of arms until the nurse opened the door.

Then when sitting happily on the bed of the nurse, she said,

"Nurse Catherine says you are going to see my little girls in America. Will you tell them something for me? Tell them Ahni is the happiest little girl in the whole world. Tell them Ahni says, 'Thank you.'"

"But," said the nurse, "if I tell them that, you must tell me why you are happy. You see they know that you have no home, and no hands and one foot. I think they would not believe me if I should tell them that. Why are you happy, Ahni?"

"Hold up your hands, nurse, so that we can count and I will tell you five reasons," said the little girl.

"First, I am happy because all the pain has been

cut away and I can sleep at night in the nice, white bed.

"Next, I have never been beaten once since I came here.

"Next, I am never hungry or cold any more.

"Next, here every one seems to love me—and no one in all the world loved me before—and here you kiss me and call me your girlie.

"And then—Oh! here I am learning to read about, and tell about, and sing about Jesus—and I love to do that.

"There are five things, nurse. Tell the little girls Ahni is the happiest little girl in all the big world. Tell them Ahni says, 'Thank you, Thank you, Thank you.' "

ON THE HILLS OF BETHLEHEM

BOGHOS, the shepherd boy, was standing on a spur of the hill that leads to Bethlehem. It was nearing night time and his sheep were gathered about him. It was in the month of December and all day long a chilly rain had been falling, so the boy felt very uncomfortable as he drew his long shepherd's cloak about him.

Boghos was an Armenian refugee from far to the north. Across his face was a deep red scar, the marks of the day when he had been torn from his mother by the Turk and brought to this land. On his body were many, many marks which told stories of suffering and cruelty. How long the three years had been!

In the happy days before the exile, Boghos had been the son of a well-to-do merchant. Their home had been different from most of the homes in the Armenian village for both father and mother had been trained in a mission school, so their home was a Christian one. They had planned great things for this one boy, now a miserable shepherd on the hills of Bethlehem.

Often in the starry night he had lain and looked at the stars and remembered the beautiful stories which his mother had told him of the the little town of Bethlehem, with the song of the angels and the birth of the little child. How little they had dreamed that he would ever tend the sheep of a

Turk on the hillsides! But here he was, miserable and cold, on this night in December.

But now his master had fled. The English had entered Jerusalem and he was no longer safe in the country. The sheep were still there and the boy had tended them, waiting to hear what he was supposed to do.

"If I keep them safely, perhaps he will let me go to the north when he comes, and then, perhaps I can find some one from home," thought the shepherd boy.

During these days since the English had entered the city, there had been a question in the mind of the boy. He had heard the other shepherds telling of the paper which General Allenby had read to the people in the old square of Jerusalem. As he had listened, he wanted to know more about it. If only he could talk to some English soldiers perhaps they could answer his questions. So he had determined to watch the road and if he saw any coming on foot, he would try to talk to them. He could speak Armenian, and Turkish, and Arabic, and a little English—surely they would be able to talk to him.

All day he had waited and watched. Some had gone flying by in automobiles; some had gone on horses. But now he was sure that the three men, whom he saw walking along the road, wore the English uniform. So turning over the care of the sheep to another boy, he went slowly to the road. Nearer and nearer came the men, and more and more nervous grew the boy, until he could only bow before them when they reached the place where he was standing. They were English soldiers. They were the ones who had come to help his people. How could he ask them his question?

Then the oldest man of the three, whose arm bore stripes for service, said kindly to him,

"What is it, boy? What can we do for you?" But the language that he used was English and only part of the sentence was understood by Boghos.

Suddenly his courage came to him and he asked in Turkish,

"Can't you talk to me in Turkish or Armenian? I do so want to know the answer to a question."

A smile lit the face of the officer as he answered, looking at the men who were with him,

"Again I am glad that I lived among the Turks," and turning to the boy he said in Turkish, "I shall be glad to answer your question. What is it?"

"Did you come with the great general?" asked the boy.

"I did," said the soldier.

"And has he brought *Him?*" said the boy eagerly.

"Brought whom, boy? I do not understand," said the officer.

"Has Jesus come back to Bethlehem? Mother told me that the Jews and the Turks had driven Him out of the land but that some day He would come back, and then we would be happy again. Mother said that He would come back when the English came. Oh, sir, I have waited so long. Have you brought Him? This is the place where He should come and it is almost His birthday. Will He come for His birthday?"—and the eyes of the boy flashed as he looked closely into the face of the English soldier.

"Do you love Him, too?" said the soldier gently,

wondering how he could ever answer the question of the boy.

"I can show you here," he answered, throwing back his cloak. "See! I have these scars on my body because I would not say I did not love Him. I could not be a Turk. I would rather die than to change. But tell me, have you brought Him back?"

The eyes of the boy seemed searching the very soul of the man. Had the English brought Him back or had they only come to protect? If he said yes, would the boy soon think he had lied. But the voice of the boy broke in again,

"Your great general said the other day that we should thank God. He said that He had come to bring peace to the land and good will among the people. He said all should have a chance. Wasn't that just what the angels sang there on the hillside so long ago? 'Glory to God in the Highest; Peace on earth, good will to men.' If He went to live in the lands to the west, as mother told me He did, can't you bring Him back? We want Him here. Please bring Him back to Bethlehem."

The soldier with the kindly face suddenly pulled the boy to a seat on a stone close to the roadside. For a moment he kicked the dirt of the road over which so many, many camel and donkey feet had passed on their way to Bethlehem. Then he said gently,

"Yes, boy, my general did say that we came to bring peace and good will, and he meant it, too. The English can't bring Jesus here, boy; but they can make it possible for Him to live here and help you all. After all these years of fighting and sorrow, you do need him. You boys with no mothers

and fathers," and he placed his hand lovingly on the
shoulder of the boy while he thought of his own
son far over the sea. "You boys need Him to make
you true, and strong, and brave.

"We can't bring Him here now, but I give you
my word of honor, boy, I will try to bring Jesus to
Bethlehem again. I shall have much to say in these
next months about what the English shall do here.
He will not come this year—it may not be next year,
but some day He will come again and then you can
all worship Him as brothers. When once again He
lives in Bethlehem, then you can help to sing as the
angels sang. I promise you, I will help all that I
can."

There were tears in the eyes of the boy as he
bent low before the soldiers and turned again to
the field. It had been so long since any one had
laid a hand lovingly on his shoulder that it almost
hurt. How kind they had been to him! The man
had reminded him of his father as he promised to
help. He was glad that he had come to them.

Slowly the three men wended their way into the
town, so full of superstition and hatred. To the old,
old church which covers the manger of Bethlehem
they went, there to see how different it all was from
the Christmas story. No wonder the boy wanted
Him to come back in all His beauty. No wonder
the boy did not love the place.

From his stone in the field the boy watched them
climb the hill to the town. Then he went to his flock
and made ready for the night. Somehow he felt
very, very lonely. Wrapping his cloak about him,
he looked for a time up into the stars which now
shone brightly. Then he bended his knee, as he had

done so many times in the old home, and he said,

"I am just a boy but I should like to help, too. Please let me help the English to bring Jesus back to Bethlehem.   We all want Him here to bring peace and good will to men."

HER ROADWAY

IT was her fiftieth birthday and Margaret Meeker lay in an easy chair looking out of the window at the beautiful flowers in the yard. Her face was white and drawn. Her hair, as it lay in ringlets about the pillow, was iron gray. Her hand moved restlessly up and down the arm of the chair. Occasionally a tear stole quietly down the sweet, gentle face. Margaret Meeker was discouraged.

She had been thinking of her fifteenth birthday. Then she was well and strong. Then she was anxious to do her very best in school so that she might fit herself for her life-work. She had consecrated her life, even then, to work in Africa. The future had been so full of promise.

And now the years had fled and her life had been so useless. Her father's death had placed on her shoulders the care of the family, and not only had she had to leave school to go to work, but she had had to give up her wonderful dream of what her life should be worth in Africa.

Then she had dreamed that perhaps she might do social service work in the city near by. But a fatal ride on a sled had brought to her the care of a sister with a broken spine. For fifteen years she had cared for her—and her vision of work for others had fled. She had been a drudge in a home rather than a worker in the field where she longed to be.

A little Sunday School class had been her only work for God in all these years.

And now the sister was dead, her own health was gone, and she was an inmate of a boarding house—lonely, in pain much of the time, discouraged. Surely her life had been very much of a failure. She had had talents, but they had been buried in a napkin. And the tears chased one another down her face. She wanted to be like the flowers in the yard; instead she had been like the weeds in the gutter—useless.

Suddenly the postman's whistle roused her from her thoughts and the kindly-faced postman stepped to the window and said,

"Here is a big one for you this morning, Miss Meeker. It looks as if it brought good news. See how it bulges at the sides."

It came from New York. It was addressed to her but she did not know the handwriting. Wearily she broke the seal and looked at the signature. Then a happy smile covered her face.

"Ah! Annie Eames!" she said. "It has been years and years since I have heard anything from her. What a dear girl she was! How hard she had to work to rise above her home! How well I remember the night when she came to tea and I gave her the new red hair-ribbon so that she might look more like the rest of the girls! I am so glad to hear from her."

Moving a bit in order to make less the pain in her body, she began to read:

"DEAR MISS MEEKER,

"I wonder if you remember me. I hope so for I want to have a real visit with you on paper. Today there has come to me a great, great honor and before I accept it, I want to write to you and give you your own big share of it all. I have been asked to lead in work for girls in one of the growing organizations in the United States and I want to thank you for it."

"To thank me! Why should she thank me?" thought the sick one.

"You will remember the little class that we had in the First Church years ago. Perhaps you will remember how very much discouraged I often was when I came to class. I was always glad to come because you always had a message for me. But one Sunday you told us a story. How well I remember it!

"You told of Robert Louis Stevenson and his kindness to the people of Samoa; of the way in which he stole into their lives through kindness and love; of the way in which he made them want to be true and peaceful because of what his life had taught them. Then you told us of the beautiful roadway which they built, making at the end a great archway on which was written words like these,

" 'Because of his kindness to us when we were sick and in prison, we have builded for Tusitala, our brother, this roadway which we have called the Road of the Loving Heart. Fame dies, honors perish but loving kindness is immortal.'

"The little story was just what I needed. I could build roadways into the lives of others even though my own life was hard. I watched you and I saw what beautiful roadways you were building into the lives of your brothers and sisters. I saw you make wonderful roadways into our lives just when we needed you most. Do you remember the red hair-ribbon? After all these years, it still lies in a box in my trunk. It was the beginning of my life of service for others. I was following you.

"I wish I could show you how beautiful the roadway is that you have built into my life. Never once have I seen you do a thoughtless thing; never once say an unkind word; never once complain. I sat often in church and watched your face, so full of patience in suffering and I prayed to be like you. Since I have left the home town, I have given myself to the work with girls—I have tried to build roadways into their lives that should be as beautiful as the one you have built into mine.

"As a result there has come to me this offer of the much larger field of service. This will give me an opportunity to touch hundreds of lives of girls every year. I am humble as I think of the task; but I am very, very grateful when I think of the opportunity it will give me. That is why I have wanted to write you the very first of all. Because you built your roadway, I have wanted to build; so you see you are really the one to whom the honor is due. As I work with the girls, it will be your spirit that is helping them to be better and nobler.

"Some day I want to come to see you if I may. I owe you *so* much and I want to look into your face and say, 'I thank you.' God help me to be the inspiration to others that your life has been to so many.

'Very sincerely your 'Girlie' as of old,
"ANNIE M. EAMES."

The letter dropped from her hand and the white face nestled into the pillow. Tear after tear rolled down her cheeks. But they were not tears of pain nor tears of discouragement. They were tears of joy. She had been of service to the world. Her life had not been useless. This was her fiftieth birthday and perhaps she could never be able to walk again, but still she could give and give. She could still build roadways into lives. She could still be patient and loving and thoughtful. She could leave to others the work in the field: she could be the inspiration, perhaps, to lives that needed her. Not in her wildest dreams had she ever hoped to reach all the lives that Annie Eames could reach in a single year's service. God had known best how to use her life and work.

Once more the light was in her face as she wrote this little note to the girl friend who lived at the foot of the street,

"I am feeling very much better. Bring some of your friends tonight and I can tell you some stories again. I have a new one which I haven't told for years and years but which I am sure you will all love to hear. I shall be so glad to tell it to you as the fire burns brightly in the fireplace and the shadows come and go."

And over and over she was saying to herself as the happy day slipped by, "Fame dies, honors perish but loving kindness is immortal."

ITS MISSION

THE studio was far up on the top floor of a great building and when one entered it, there was little to tell one of the greatness of the man who worked there. The floor was littered with bits of glass, putty and lead. All seemed to be disorder and confusion.

Very early one morning a boy entered the studio bearing in his hands a basket containing bits of glass. Very carefully he laid them on the table and turned to leave the room. But as he turned, his basket caught a tiny piece of glass and swept it to the floor. He tried to find it; then the ringing of a bell caused him to leave the room and the glass was forgotten.

But it was only a piece of glass so what did it matter. It had little of beauty for it was jagged and rough. It was small and lacking in color, so no one noticed it all through the day. It was kicked by the messenger boy; it was brushed aside by the maid; finally, several days later, it found itself in a pile of rubbish, ready to be carried to the street.

Now the bit of glass had had dreams of greatness when it had been chosen by the Master. It had dreams of some day being a part of a great window in a beautiful church. So, as it found itself being pushed further and further into the corner, it said to itself,

"Oh, dear, I had hoped to be of some use somewhere. How dreadful it will be to be thrown out

into the street with old bottles and bits of glass!
I am sure the Master meant me for some good use
for He was so careful in choosing me. I wonder
if there isn't any way by which I can be found. If
some one comes this way, I shall prick. If the sunshine comes in the corner, I shall shine. But there
seems to be nothing else that I can do. I will try
for I do not want to be thrown away."

So it glistened as best it could—but no one saw.
It turned its sharp corners straight up—but no one
came near.

After some days the Master came to the studio
and began to work. He drew aside a homely cur-
tain that was pulled across the rear of the room and
the sunshine streamed through a wonderful window
upon which he was working. In the lower part of
the window there were many, many little children
and they were looking up and smiling. All about
them were flowers. Above the children was the
figure of a man, as yet incomplete.

With a happy smile, the artist seated himself
before the picture. He looked long at the work he
had already done. Then he began to put in the
pieces of glass which had been laid on the table.
There was a red piece that finished the robe of the
man. Other bits of glass made his hand.

The little bit of glass in the corner heard him
talking to himself as he worked.

"This is to be my very best," he said. "So many,
many months I have worked to make this window.
It must tell to the world how much I love the Christ.
It must be beautiful to show His beauty. If only I
can make it tell what I feel, how glad I shall be."
And he sang as he worked.

The days went by, and as friends stood beside the artist and talked to the artist, the bit of glass in the corner knew that the window was almost completed. And because it knew this, more and more plainly came the thought,

"I was mistaken. There is no place for me in the window. I shall never be missed. I cannot help to show the beauty of the Christ to the world. There is no place for me in the plan of the artist."

Suddenly there was a commotion in the studio. The artist went from one place to another looking for something. The boy was sent for and questioned. Then he was sent to the factory to see if he could find what had been lost. The table was moved; the books were moved; the floor was carefully swept. And the glass heard the artist say,

"I can't finish without it. It was such a wonderful piece and I had spent so much time and thought on it. Where can it be? I just must have it to finish the window. I must have it." ·

Then the bit of glass in the corner began to dream again.

"Can it be I? Could I be an important part of the window? Will the picture be spoiled if I am not there? Did he make me carefully for a special place? Oh, I hope so! I hope some one will find me. All I can do is to shine. I will catch the beam of sunshine that is stealing across the floor and perhaps some one will see me shine."

So the bit of glass did its best—and the sunshine helped it to sparkle and gleam.

There was a cry of delight, and the bit of glass was pulled from the rubbish pile where it had lain with other useless things. It was laid in the hand

of the Master and turned over and over to see if it
had been harmed by its contact with common things.
Then it was polished and carried to the window.

A placing of the glass, a bit of leading, and lo!
the bit of glass which others had thought useless and
not beautiful was the eye of the Christ of the window. The rough places found just their companion
pieces and the color gleamed in the light.

Carefully the artist put it into its place. Eagerly
he watched to see what story it would tell. And
when he stepped away and looked into the face of
the Christ, the eye was full of tenderness, and love,
and compassion. It told to the world of the love of
the artist for the Christ.

And the bit of glass—ah! it went out into the
world, into the niche of the great and beautiful
church. It was one of the smallest most unattrac-
tive bits of glass in the whole window when left by
itself, but when used in the way that the Master
meant it should be, it became the heart of the
window.

To those who looked into the window when they
were sad, it brought comfort; to those who were
lonely, it brought a message of friendship; to the
children, it told of the love of the Master.

To all who looked into the window there came
a message of love and of beauty. The bit of glass
had found its place—and was content.

HIS FIRST OFFENSE

JOHN STANLEY, a well-to-do business man of forty-five, had been sent for to come to the city jail. A prisoner has asked to see him. So, very reluctantly, he was on his way there. He hated the jail. For days and days after he had been there he could see the dirty, fighting crowd in the "pen." It hurt him to see people being punished, for he had a kind and generous heart.

Down the dark stairs he went with the orderly, waited before the barred window while the orderly called the name of the man who had asked him to come. Then as he waited, he saw a boy.

He was about fifteen years old. His clothes were torn and very, very dirty. One sleeve hung in tatters. His straight hair, black as a coal, fell over his forehead, showing that it had been cut by some one who knew little about it. His face was white and—oh! so frightened. He cowered in the corner, afraid of the drunken men, afraid of the crazy man who screamed in the cell near by, afraid most of all of what was to happen to him. And as John Stanley looked into his face, the great, wondering eyes seemed to haunt him.

"Why is that little fellow in here? Is there no place where he can be with boys, instead of in this howling, ill-smelling place? Surely he has committed no crime," he said to the attendant.

"He was brought in night-before-last with a gang

of boys who were trying to break into a store," said
the attendant. "He looks innocent enough but you
can never tell. He was with them so he must take
his punishment with the rest. He belongs to that
bunch playing cards over there but he has nothing to
do with them. We have no other place but this for
prisoners. It is his first offense so of course he is
frightened."

All of the time that he was talking to the man
who had sent for him, John Stanley's eyes were on
the face of the boy who stood so still and whose
thoughts seemed so far away. Oh, how he pitied
him! Suppose it had been Billy, his boy! Yet
something might happen to bring him here. He was
always getting into mischief with the boys. And
John Stanley felt a cold shudder pass over him as
he thought of the things the boy would hear, the
harm that would be done him by days spent in the
jail.

An hour later he was trying to free him. The boy
had had no chance to explain why he had been near
the boys, so he was brought before the judge with
his great eyes full of fear and shame. What would
they do to him? He told him of the way the boys
had taken his money and then forced him to watch
on the corner. They lived in his neighborhood and
had said they would fight him if he did not do as
he was told. There was no question that he was
innocent. Yet he had been arrested under the law.
It was his first offense.

A little influence, a little insistence—then the pay-
ment of the fine and the business man went to the
pen to get the little fellow. He took him to the
home on the hill, gave him a warm bath, brought out

some of the clothes that Billy had outgrown and when he came back to the library, he seemed like a new boy. Together they ate the supper which tasted so good after the days on prison fare.

Then Mr. Stanley asked him about his home. He had wanted to get rid of the look of fear before he took him home to his mother.

"I haven't any home, sir," said the boy. "Mother died a year ago and father just went off and left me. Most of the time I sleep in boxes and alleys. But when it rains, I stay out until I have sold enough papers to get a bed in the newsboy's home. And I have no money now for those boys took every bit of it. But I guess tomorrow the paper-man will trust me for he knows I wouldn't cheat him. I know where I can sleep tonight all right. I thank you, sir. I just thank you more than you know. I hope I never have to go back in that awful place again."

The boy started for his hat. But Mr. Stanley had been thinking. A customer had told him some time before that she wanted a boy to come into her home and live and help with the fires, errands, etc. He told Robert about her and then talked with the lady herself on the telephone. She still wanted a boy, so soon they were on their way to her home.

And Robert, the prisoner, became Bob, the helper. In school he was called by the name of the lady in whose home he lived and so his new life just blotted out his old name altogether.

Mr. Stanley had promised to be a big brother to him and he was. But in a year, the place of his business was changed to a distant state and so the two drifted apart. To Mr. Stanley it had been only one of the many kindly things which he had been able to do.

Twenty years passed by; the war came; business reverses followed; Billy, the son, was killed in France and his mother died soon afterward. Then John Stanley, the broken, homeless man, searched for a place to work. His home was only a lodging house; his friends had forgotten that he had ever lived, apparently. No work was to be had in his own business—he was too old to begin anew. He was totally discouraged as he tramped the streets day after day.

One morning there came a telegram from an old friend saying that a new corporation was to be formed and he was needed. So, gladly, he went to their office, looked over their plans, seemed to see great prospects ahead. He was to be field worker for the concern and he threw himself into the work with all his might. Orders piled into the office and he seemed on the way once more to success.

As he was looking over the mail one morning, three policemen came into the office, produced a warrant, and arrested him for swindling the public. They took him to the jail and, without a chance to defend himself, they placed him in the pen with drunken men, with gamblers and with men of ill-fame. How he shrank from them all! It seemed to him as if the hours were days. Who would defend him? He had no money. Why did not his partners come to release him? They knew that he was innocent of any wrong.

That very same morning, a famous lawyer in a distant city was reading his paper when he saw in big headlines,

"John Stanley arrested for swindling the public. Has been a prominent citizen for many years. This is his first offense against the law."

The paper dropped from his hands. "John Stanley!" He must go at once to the help of his friend. But if he went he would anger the men who were pushing him for election to the office of the district attorney. Perhaps he would lose the election. He dropped his head on the table in thought, then ordered his car, and was soon on his way to the distant city.

. He came to the court asking to be allowed to defend the man, stated that he had heard that he had no money and it would be a pleasure to work for him. He also asked that the prisoner simply be told that Lawyer Roundley had been assigned to the case. Then he began his work. He interviewed the prisoner carefully, he sought evidence everywhere. The partners had left the country and so there was no one to refute the claim that the firm had not meant to swindle in the claims which they had made. It was a hard fight for there was much evidence against him. But, little by little, the brilliant lawyer won his points. Carefully he made his appeal for leniency, and John Stanley was freed.

With his arm in that of the lawyer, the prisoner led the way to the little room at the rear. Then he said sadly,

"Mr. Roundley, I do not know what was told you before you took my case. I have not a cent of money in the world. But I appreciate more than I can tell you all the hard fight you have made for my freedom. Some day I shall pay you all—every

cent. Will you send to me your bill for your services."

Then a smile broke over the face of the lawyer
as he turned about and said,

"Does an older brother need to thank a younger
brother for giving him his freedom? I also had a
first offense. I also had a stranger who came to my
aid. I have only repaid my debt." And he held
out his hand to the astonished man.

"Years make a lot of changes, don't they?" he
said. "You see you never knew my old name which
I took again when I went to college. I was sure
that you would not know me. And now let us hurry
home. Mary is anxious to see my only brother."

So the little brother took the older brother to
the distant city where none knew him; a warm bath
removed the stain of the days in prison; new clothes
were ready in his room so that he might feel like a
new man. Then, together, they sought the nursery
where a sweet-faced woman was getting a little
fellow ready for bed. It was a warm welcome that
she gave to the man who had given her husband his
chance to make good. It was a happy man who
joined the family circle for the evening meal.

And as they talked together during the evening,
the older brother found that the younger brother
needed some one to advise him, some one to help
him in the office, some one to attend to things when
he was away from home. There was a place where
he could help. He could retrieve the good name
which he had lost.

So he began his new life and in no time at all John
Stanley, the prisoner, had become Grandaddy Jack
to the ruler of the Roundley household.

FOR MOTHER

OVER the steep slope of the Lebanon mountains the great automobile pushed its way. It
zigzagged here and there; occasionally it stopped at
some of the small towns in order that the passengers might buy the luscious plums, or grapes, which
the natives had for sale.

The day was very, very hot and the road was very
dusty, but both were forgotten because of the wonderful view on every side. Great rocky cliffs, deep,
deep valleys, quaint little hamlets were everywhere.
The tops of the mountains were in the clouds and,
here and there, a patch of snow could be seen.

The people along the roadway, too, were interesting. Many camel drivers walked slowly behind
heavily loaded camels. On their backs were great
sacks of grain or charcoal; natives pushed along the
little donkeys loaded with produce brought from the
city in the valley; children with black, black skins,
burned by the sun, ran beside the automobile asking
for pennies. They looked very thin and very poor,
for the war had been long in their land.

Only one of the passengers seemed to be thinking
of something else than the things along the way.
She was a young American girl, a tourist who had
for several weeks been seeing the interesting things
in the cities of Europe and the Near East. Today
her mind was full of questioning. Everywhere she

had been seeing the wonderful strings of amber beads—so tempting to any woman, but especially so to a girl. In her pocket she carried money which she could spend for the trip. She had wanted some of the beads ever since she had seen the first ones. Should she get them?

They were expensive but not nearly so expensive as they would be in America. They would last her all through her life as a memento of the trip. No other girl would have such ambers. How proud she would be to show them and tell where she had bought them! All the girls would envy her.

But if she bought them, it would take most of the money that she had planned for her friends. Ought she not to take things home to the rest after having spent all the money needed for the trip on herself? What should she do? Over and over she turned the question in her mind. Soon they would be at Damascus and here she would be able to get beautiful ones in the oldest city in the world. So in her mind she was trying to decide the question as she rode up the mountainside.

Then came a bit of the way through the clouds, a laugh at the snow bank close to the road side, and before them lay the valley of the Bekkah, one of the most beautiful valleys in the world. Surely they must stop and look for a time.

As the strangers stepped from the automobile, the children came running from all directions. Some lived in the little villages near by; some lived in the little, black Bedouin tents made of camel-hair. All were dirty, and black, and noisy, as they crowded around the strangers.

Most of the party moved to the right but the

American girl and a friend went apart a bit to an overhanging rock. In her hand she carried a beautiful pear which she had purchased in the valley, and which she had been polishing as she came up the mountainside. It was large and perfect. It looked as if it would be very, very good to eat.

Suddenly she noticed that one starved-looking little girl had left the others and was standing close to her, looking so longingly at the pear. Her face was so full of hunger, and she seemed to be trying to smell the beautiful fruit. Smilingly the girl held it toward her but the little body drew back.

"Would you like it?" said the dragoman who was in charge of the party, speaking in Arabic. "You may have it if you like."

"I should love to have it," she answered. "It is so beautiful."

"Are you hungry?" asked the girl, and the dragoman interpreted her words to the little one.

"I am always hungry," she said. "The fields are bare this year and there is never much to eat."

She took the pear in her hands and turned it over and over. She rubbed it against her cheek; she patted it with her hand; she had forgotten the strangers in her joy at owning the pear. Quietly they watched her and the minutes passed. Then, lifting it to her mouth, she took the tiniest bite close to the stem, but only one. Folding it close in her dirty apron so that the others might not see it, she started to go.

"Why don't you eat the pear?" asked the girl. "Don't you like it? I thought you said you were hungry."

"I am hungry," said the little girl, "but the pear

I am going to give to my mother. She never has
anything like this. She will like it so much and I
can make her eyes shine as I give it to her. Then
she will have something that none of the others
have. I should like to eat it but I want to give it to
her. I love my mother."

The eyes of the American girl were wet as she
said sweetly,

"Come with me, Zalpha, I think I can find another one. It may not be as big but it is just as
good."

So they went to the car and found more fruit in
the basket there.

"Let me see you eat this one," said the older girl.
"Then you may take the big one to mother."

The teeth of the little Bedouin bit hastily into the
pear and she ate it so greedily that there was no
doubt of her hunger. A sandwich and an apple
were brought from the car and these, too, were
eaten. Then with a look which showed how full
of thanks her little heart was, she hurried across the
fields toward one of the black tents.

The automobile started on its way and the girl
in the back seat watched eagerly to see her enter
the tent. Looking back, after they had made another sharp turn in the road, she saw the mother
and the daughter standing on the hill, watching
the car disappear from view.

A few days later the party entered the old, old
city of Damascus. Down the long bazaar-streets
they went, admiring the beautiful silks, the carefully-
made brass utensils and all the odd, odd things
found only in Syria. But the girl of the party made

her way to the part of the bazaars where the amber was to be found.

"So you have decided to buy a string of the beads, have you?" asked her friend.

"Yes, I want a very beautiful string," said the girl. "I want to take them to mother. She has nothing so beautiful as these will be and I can make her eyes shine as I give them to her. Then she will have something that none of the other mothers have and she will know how much I love her. I should like to have them myself but I want to give them to her. I love that little mother of mine over the sea so I am going to take her ambers which she can always have to enjoy."

And that is why a mother in America fingers lovingly a string of ambers as they hang about her neck and says often to herself, "I am so happy with them because they show how very much she must love me."

THE LEGEND OF THE WINGS

(PERSIAN)

O NCE in the long ago, before man came to the earth to live, the birds had sweet voices with which to sing; they had beautiful colors with which to make the roadways bright, but they had no wings. They hopped about from place to place, often in danger of their lives from the animals all about them, but they could not fly.

Now there was work to be done in the animal world and God chose one and another of the animals and birds to do it. Some scattered seeds, some carried messages, some worked to make the world more beautiful. But none of the animals wished to bear burdens from one place to another.

The lion said, "I am too great to carry bundles."

The rabbit said, "I am too small to carry bundles."

The sheep said, "I give wool so why should I carry bundles?"

The chipmunk said, "I must run fast and far so how can I carry bundles?"

One and another they all asked to be excused— all but the birds. When they saw that the bundles had to be carried, they said to the great God who guarded them,

"We are very small and cannot carry much. But we are glad to do what we can. Make the bundles small and we can help to do the work. There are many of us; perhaps we can do it all."

So the bundles were put on their backs. Sometimes they staggered under the weight of them but still they carried; and they sang their sweet songs as they hopped along. They could still pick up bits of food as they went along. At first their songs could not be understood, but gradually the other animals found that they were singing,

"Never mind about the burdens. We will do our very best."

And as the days went by, the burdens seemed lighter. Soon the burdens seemed to be lifting them instead of their lifting the burdens. Then lo! when the winter was over and the springtime came again, the burdens rolled away and in their place were wings—wings with which they could fly away from danger and spend their days in the beautiful sky and in the tree-tops. They had learned how to carry the burden, and the burden had become wings to lift them nearer to the great God for whom they had done the work.

MARJORY'S GIFT

IT was a hot July morning and the summer sun seemed as if it would burn whatever it touched. The children sat in the doorways, not caring to play; the mothers worked eagerly in order to get the work of the home done before it should get any hotter.

In one of the doorways sat Marjory but she was not worrying about the heat. She was just waiting for a half hour to pass and then she could go down to the church on the next block and spend the morning in the Vacation Bible School. The church had such big, brick walls and such big, big rooms that it was always cool there in the morning, no matter how hot the day might be. So every day Marjory took her sisters and one brother there for the morning.

Marjory was so happy in the Vacation School. She liked the sewing and the hammock-making; she liked the singing and the marching; but best of all, she liked the stories which the teachers told. Every night she would tell them over and over to the children at home and every day she waited eagerly for the time to come when she should hear a new one.

Yesterday the teacher had told of a little African girl named Bunga who had given her beautiful, red beads of which she was very proud so that a missionary might be sent to her town to teach her mother the things which she had been wanting to hear.   And when Bunga had given the beads, she had said,

"If they will send a missionary to my mother to make her happy, then I give them with all my heart."   Marjory could just see Bunga's eyes shine and her lips smile as she gave the beads.   When the teacher had finished the story, Marjory had thought to herself,

"Oh, dear, I wish I had something to give to make others better and happier.   But I never have anything to give.   I never have anything that others would want.   I should like to give like Bunga."

As she had told the story again to the children at night, the thought had come again,

"I wish I had something to give.   I should like to say to some one, "Then I give it with all my heart."

So it was Bunga of whom she was thinking as she sat on the doorstep of her home on that hot July morning.   What could she give?   She was only twelve years old.   Maybe she would have to wait until she was as old as the teacher who had told the story.   Then she could earn some money to give, at least.   That would be better than never to give at all.

Suddenly she saw the ambulance stop in front of a little house down the street.   That was where Mrs. Allen lived with her five children.   Down the street Marjory hurried and waited to see what was to happen.   Soon the stretcher was carried out of the house with John, the oldest boy, on it.   He was crying as loud as ever he could and begging his mother not to leave him.

"No, Sonny, Mother can't go for there is no one

to stay with the children," said the mother. "The doctors will be so good to you and they will make you all well again in a little while. Be a little man and help mother by going bravely as you said you would," said the mother, her face white with suffering. With the tears streaming down her face, she kissed him good-by again, but he fought to get up from the stretcher unless she would go.

Suddenly a little voice said to Marjory,

"You know those little children well. You could play with them for the morning and let the mother go to the hospital with John."

"But it is so hot," thought Marjory. "Then, too, I have to go to school in a few minutes. I couldn't miss school."

"I thought you were looking for something to give to help another. Didn't the teacher say that the very biggest thing one had to give was oneself?" insisted the voice.

"It is too hot to play with children," said Marjory to herself. "If I stayed here I should miss the story at school and I don't want to do that."

And once more the voice said,

"I thought you really wanted to give but I guess you didn't."

They put the stretcher into the ambulance and the driver jumped to the seat. The little fellow was still begging for his mother to come and Marjory saw Mrs. Allen put her fingers in her ears and then start to hurry into the house. For a moment she still hesitated. Then she touched Mrs. Allen on the shoulder and said,

"You go with John, Mrs. Allen. The children like to play with me and I will take good care of them until you get back again. I can stay here until I have to take father's dinner at noon."

"May the good Lord bless you for being kind to us," said the mother and away she went in the ambulance.

Then Marjory went into the little house. The dishes weren't even washed and there were so many of them piled high in the kitchen. But she taught the children to play a "dish game" with her and soon they were done and in their places. Then she swept the floor and made the beds. By this time it was nearly ten o'clock and very, very hot.

The easiest place in which to keep them contented was at the playground, so she started with the four children following close as could be. Oh, how hot it was! Over and over she compared it with the cool rooms at the church. The children, who were at the playground when they reached it, were already cross and so the morning was a very uncomfortable one for them all. Sometimes she was almost discouraged but she remembered the way in which Bunga had given her gift.

"If it is to be a real gift, I must give it with all my heart," she said.

So she played, and jumped, and slid down the coaster, and taught them every game that she knew. When the clock struck eleven Marjory remembered that it was time for the story at the Vacation School and how she did want to be there! Suddenly a happy thought came to her. Why not tell a story to the children while the teacher at the school was telling hers? It would be such fun.

Quickly she gathered as many children as she could over in one of the corners of the playground where it was shady. She made them sit in a circle just as they did at school. Then she sat on a box before them and began.

First she told them of how a good fairy searched all over the land for a good boy and finally found him in a little house away down in a back alley. When this story was finished, Marjory's face was covered with smiles for more children had come t) the corner and dropped to the ground. Then she told them of Pig Brother and as she told it, the little hands began wiping the dirt from their faces lest a little pig should walk through the playground and claim some one of them for its brother.

Her teacher had said one day that three stories made just enough for a group of children to hear in an hour. She had just time to tell another. She thought of all that she knew and then decided that she must tell them of the little girl with the red beads. So she borrowed a string of red beads that one of the girls had about her neck (for she must tell it just as Miss Jones had told it to her). She loved that story so she was sure she could tell it well.

How eagerly they listened to her! She could see it all so plainly that she made them see it, too, and when she had finished, they loved little Bunga and wanted to be like her, also.

The whistle was blowing and Marjory rose quickly to take the children home, and then take a dinner basket to her father. As she turned, she found herself looking into the eyes of the story-lady of the Vacation School.

"I had to leave early today. I was passing the playground when I saw this little group in the corner. It looked so interesting that I had to come in.

I heard a bit of the story which you were telling to them so very nicely. Then the worker in the playground told me that you had given your whole morning to the care of the Allen children while the mother went to the hospital. We missed you at school, but I am so glad you had a gift to give this morning when one was so much needed. I think, by your eyes as you told the story, that you must be like Bunga. I am sure you gave it with all your heart. You have helped the mother and John, but you have also helped all these little children on this very, very hot day. That is much to give, girlie."

So the happy little girl went back to the house. Mrs. Allen was there to care for the children and when she thanked the little caretaker and told her how much she had helped, Marjory knew that even though she didn't have money or pretty things, still she had something that was very much worth while to give to help others. She had learned the happiness of giving with all her heart.

HER FATHER'S DAUGHTER

WITHIN the old town of Zaragoza in Spain there was great confusion. For many, many weeks the French had been besieging the town without gaining ground. Now they seemed determined to force the surrender. They had massed all their strength on one side of the wall and, one by one, the men guarding it had been killed or wounded.

The air was thick with smoke; the shots whizzed through the air; the wounded were everywhere. But the worst of the confusion was on the wall. The brave old gunner in command of the big gun had been wounded and lay at the bottom of a pile of men. There was no one to man the gun, and the French had a clear road into that part of the city. The men called for help but their voices were drowned in the noise from without.

Suddenly a voice was heard, "Father, Father, where are you? I cannot see for the smoke. Are you wounded? I have come with water and bandages."

The men lifted their heads for they knew the voice. It was the Maid of Zaragoza, as they called her. It was the daughter of the old gunner—the heroine of the siege. How many times they had seen her come to help on the wall! She had brought water when their throats seemed burning with the powder. She had carried messages when they could not be spared from the fort. She had even shot

off the big gun in her father's place in order to give
him rest. How they all loved her!

Groping along through the dense smoke, she
came, only to find the big gun silent and her father
nowhere to be found.

"Father! Father!" she called again, eagerly.
Bending low to search for him, she saw a hand
being lifted above the rest, and a head moving
slowly back and forth. In the hand she saw a
match.

"Argostina—fire—the gun," he said faintly, and
then he was gone.

With a cry of pain the girl fled to the gun. Down
the roadway she could see the lines of the French
making for the wall. The big gun had been silent
so long that they thought it safe to come nearer.
Should she let them take her city? Never! The
flames from below sent burning heat into her face;
a bullet flew very close to her head. But quietly she
made ready and then——

A noise, a burst of light, a shriek of pain, and the
French fell in great numbers in the path of the gun.
Dumb with surprise, the men waited and then heard
the command to retreat. Evidently there were still
plenty of men to guard the fort. And away they
went.

Then Argostina bent low beside the father who
had been so dear to her. How much she loved him!
She looked into his powder-marred face and strok-
ing it gently, she said,

"You gave me your gun, father dear, and I shall
not leave it until Zaragoza is saved. I shall stay
here until death or victory shall come."

And there the commander found her, after the

men had told him of her brave deed. There he found her again the next morning, cleaning the big gun as if it were her very own.

"Father gave it into my keeping the very last thing," she said. "May I not man it until the end of the siege? I know how to do it and I am not afraid. May I have the gun and draw my father's pay so that his little ones in the home may not lack for food? My father would have trusted me with the gun if he had been here."

The commander looked into the dark, thoughtful eyes of the girl who had saved the fort. It was a man's task but she could do it. Then he said,

"Your wish is granted. You may prove that you are your father's daughter. You may man the gun."

The days that came were hard and long. But she was brave and loyal, and never for a moment did she falter. Her courage kept the men to their task, and when they would have surrendered the fort, she was still true to her post.

Finally there came a day when it seemed as if they surely must surrender. It seemed useless to try to hold out longer. A council was being held to determine what to do. Suddenly some one called out,

"Ask the Maid of Zaragoza. I will abide by her answer." The crowd took up the cry, and away went the messenger of the commander to the wall where the girl was standing.

She listened to the question. Then placing her right hand tenderly on her father's gun and looking far, far away as though she might see him, she said,

"We will never surrender. It shall be war to the knife."

So when relief came, they found the little town still holding out against the enemy. After the French had fled the commander himself brought to her the medal of honor and pinned it on her dress saying,

"To you the people of Zaragoza owe their freedom. You have been brave and courageous, strong and true. You are your father's own daughter. For love of him and love of country you have shown your heroism. We love you and we honor you."

A SECOND PETER

GREAT headlines in the paper had told the story of the operation. His picture had been sent all over the country. On Tuesday he had been a surgeon in a little town in the hills of Vermont. Then suddenly he had become famous. Wednesday found him a great hero.

There had been a wreck on the railroad. He had been a passenger on the train; he had helped to carry the wounded to the hospitals; he had forgotten his own bruises in helping others. Then, because another surgeon had not been available at the moment and a life had been at stake, he had been asked to operate. There was only one chance in a hundred that the injured man could live—but John Barrie had taken that chance in hand and won.

The papers had told of his clear directions at the time of the accident; of his steady hand; of his iron nerve as he worked, hour after hour, cutting, fitting, replacing the wounded parts. He had done that which had never before been so successfully done in the annals of surgery.

Mothers had read the story and blessed him for saving the life of the great man whom they had learned to love and trust. Surgeons had read the story and marveled. Young men and boys had read the story and wished that they might just take the hand of a man who could do such wonderful things.

But the hero of the hour, John Barrie, sat in his

office at the close of the week writing, hour after hour, on large sheets of paper. He was trying to do what he had been asked by one of the medical journals to do for them—write an account of his training; his life of service; his story of the operation; the difficulties which he had had to overcome in order to make it a success. At the close of the paper, he had been asked to state the three things in life which he felt sure had contributed most to his success as a surgeon.

So he had written the story of his school days, his struggle for an education, his first field of practice. Then he had written of the accident; he had told in detail what he had done, feeling that perhaps it might help others to save life also. He had told of the devotion of the nurses, the coöperation of the doctors and the strength of body found in the patient. To write all this had been comparatively easy.

Then he had come to the statement of what, in his opinion, had contributed most to his success.

For more than an hour he had worked on that statement. At first, he had written down all the things that it might be: health, friends, grit, hard work, etc. Then, one by one, he had crossed out the least important words from the list. At last he had only three words left. But could he be sure that these were the three things which he wanted to say? Once more he read them over before putting them on the typewritten sheets:

"A trained mind, a steady nerve, and confidence in my own ability to do the work."

Yes, those three things had given him the victory. He was very sure of it. So with a great sigh of relief, he leaned back in his chair to rest for a moment. As he did so, he saw on the wall a picture of a woman.

"Ah," he said with a smile, "how proud mother would have been to have read—" and then he stopped, stunned by a new thought that had come to him.

Never once in all of these pages and pages had he given her one bit of credit for his success. Never once! To whom did he owe his trained mind? The details of the room faded away and he was again a boy of fourteen. He saw her in her faded black dress working long hours, day after day, in order that he might go to high school. He saw her helping him, night after night, with his lessons in order that he might keep his place at the head of the class, thereby winning a coveted medal. He heard her showing him how to push ahead in his studies.

He saw her on his graduation day from the high school. Her eyes were shining and she was saying,

"John, somehow you must go on. You have a good mind and can make a name for yourself. We will work together, you and I. No matter what it costs either of us, you must go on. I owe it to you. I want to give it to you."

Then he saw her being a mother to many, many boys in a boarding house just off the campus during the four years at college. He felt again her hand on his shoulder and heard her say,

"I wouldn't slight my work, John. Every bit of it will help you in the days that are ahead. Make every day count."

Then he saw the boys coming to say good-by to her and he heard one of them say,

"I wish you were my mother. John Barrie ought to do some great thing in life after living with you all these years. I envy him his chance."

To whom did he owe his education? To himself? His paper had told of his struggles to get that education; but was it he that had really had the hard struggle in order that he might know how to cut on that day of the accident? If she had not been a real mother, would he have known how to have done the work? He knew in his soul that he had not told the truth.

But how could he say this in a paper which was to go out to the press? They wanted to know how *he* had won fame. Could he change it a bit and show that she, also, had helped him to win? He picked up the paper, read a few paragraphs to see where he should insert the new sentences—and his eye caught that second statement of fact: "A steady nerve."

Who was responsible for that steady nerve? Did he win that by practice alone? The question carried him back again to boyhood days. He was seventeen years of age and was walking through the woods with a kindly-faced man of forty. He had been telling the man of his dreams some day to be a great surgeon. He had been planning with him how he could earn money enough to go through college and then to the medical school. As they walked, he pulled from his pocket a cigarette case and offered one to his friend. Then he heard him say,

"I can't afford to smoke one of those. In my work at the factory I have to have a steady hand, and that would steal away the power to do the thing which I have to do. A surgeon needs the steadiest hand of any man in the world, for he has the lives of loved ones in his hand. If I were you, I would throw that case into the pond and never buy another. It will hurt your chances of success, John. You can't afford to use cigarettes any more than I can."

He saw that man showing him how to keep from the temptations that came to other boys in college; he saw again some of the letters which had come to him in college showing that the man expected him to be strong and true. He felt again the thrill of the days which he had spent in that man's home after his dear mother had died. Ah! how much he owed to that man! Left alone to fight the battle at seventeen, would he have come to this day with a steady hand and an iron nerve? Never! He knew only too well how strong the temptations had been. It had been the friendship, the counsel, and the faith of this man which had kept him steady.

But how could he tell the world of his reason for having a steady hand? It would make lips curl and faces grow scornful if he should say that he owed it to the influence of a good friend and teacher. Surely he must leave that last statement out of his paper. He could never send it as it was, for it was not the truth. Neither could he afford to tell the truth now that his chance for a great name was at stake. "Confidence in my own ability to do the work." The words stared him in the face as he picked up the sheets of paper, thinking that he would put them away until another day.

Had he been confident when they had told him who the injured man was? Had he not felt faint when they had told him that he must do the work? Yet he had walked with steady step when he had

entered the operating room. Whence had come the
confidence? Dared he tell them that he had bowed
his head and asked for help as soon as the nurse
had left the room? Dared he tell the world of the
influence of the old, old story of Gideon, which his
mother had told him years and years before when a
very hard choice had come to him? Could he own
to others that that very morning as he had walked
down the corridor he had heard again the promise
of the old story,

"Go in this thy might! Have I not sent thee?
Surely I will be with thee."

Would the world still think that he was great if
they knew that the confidence which they had admired came to him from God? This was not necessary for surgeons to know. Ah! but the paper
would be on the shelves of the medical schools, and
it would be a good thing for the young men to know.
For which group should he write? The perspira-
tion stood out in great drops on his forehead as he
fought his way through the maze of thoughts which
were filling his mind.

And even as he fought, he saw *Him*.

He, John Barrie, was seated with the surgeons,
and again Jesus, the Christ, was on trial. Slowly he
passed through the room where the men sat and as
he passed, he looked at John with a smile of love
and sympathy. But ringing through the air, John
Barrie heard, in no uncertain tones, three words,

"A second Peter!   A second Peter!"

He bowed his head on the desk while his face
burned with shame. He had tried to make of himself a hero at the cost of his mother, his friend and
his God. Five long minutes passed before the head

was again lifted. Slowly his hand reached out before him until it touched the frame of a picture which stood on his desk. Long he looked into the gentle face which was pictured there. Then he said tenderly,

"That which you gave to me as a boy, I still want to keep. More than anything else in the whole world, I want to have *You* proud of me—to think me a hero. I will rewrite the paper."

For the next hours his pen fairly flew. He told of his mother's love and sacrifice, and of his struggle to be worthy of her love and trust. He told of the help of his friend, and the gratitude of his heart for the ideal of manhood which that friend had helped to raise in his life. He told of the days of service in the little town and of the accident. He told of his fight for the life of his patient. Then, with a rare smile on his face, he wrote:

"My success is due to three things, I am sure:

a. To a wonderful mother who taught me to value a trained mind and to love to study and to think.

b. To a good friend who taught me how to keep clean and true; who taught me the results of foolish habits on my life and so helped me to be able to have, in manhood, a steady nerve and a body in control of my will.

c. To a God who has allowed me to believe that I work with Him and for Him in trying to save life and lift burdens, thus creating within me a confidence in His help in times of great need.

JOHN BARRIE."

The paper was sealed, mailed and sent on its way. Mothers read it—and into their hearts came a great happiness that it was given to them to help to give great heroes and helpers to the world. Surgeons read it—and wondered at the humility of the man. Boys and young men read it—and wished even more that they might take the hand of John Barrie and hold it fast within their own as they struggled toward their future. The man whose life he had saved read the paper and said thoughtfully, "No wonder! Now I understand."

So John Barrie became a second Peter as he conquered his own self—and so was able to become a fisher, as well as a healer, of men.

THE ROYAL ERRAND

THE old, gray castle, high on the cliffs, looked stern and forbidding as the young knight rode swiftly toward it in the early dawn. The sun was just pushing its head up over the brow of the hill, touching the earth here and there with tints of red and yellow. But none of the light touched the castle. It was so dark and still that the knight almost hesitated to pull the great bell-rope and announce his coming.

He was clad in full armor; he rode on a coal-black charger; he had come at the call of the king, —he was eager to serve, for he was brave and true.

The draw-bridge was lowered; the great gate swung open and his face glowed with pride as he heard one announce: "The messenger of the King comes! Tell ye our Lord, the King."

His great horse pawed the ground with impatience as they waited. Like his master, he was eager to be away over hills and valley in search of adventure.

Then a trumpet announced the coming of the king, and the knight raised his helmet and bowed low before him. He loved this master. He longed to show that love by deeds well done,—by a life of service.

In silence they rode together through the court-yard to the great gate of the castle. In his hand the King bore a roll of parchment. His face seemed very grave and sad. "Surely," thought the knight, "This is to be a sacred task that he is to give me. Ah! that he should have chosen me. I am honored by the call."

As they came to the drawbridge, the King halted. Looking the knight full in the face, he said,

"Art thou ready to ride forth for me, Sir Knight?"

"Aye, sire, I am ready and eager," he answered.

"Behold, here is a message which I would send unto all my people. It is for great and small; it is for rich and poor. It will bring blessings unto all. Guard it well. Wilt thou do this, Sir Knight?"

"I will, sire. I will guard it with my life and honor," answered the knight.

"Dost thou carry any needless burden? Swiftly must thou ride in order that all may hear," said the King.

"I bear no burden that is not necessary. I have laid them all aside. I shall ride fast and far as the day breaks over the hill," said the knight.

"Then ride on—carry my message. But stay— many shall say to thee as thou ridest, 'Sir Knight, come here and see.' Maidens will call to thee; gay things will beckon thee; perchance even war shall claim thy help. But unto all these things thou shalt say,

" '*Stand aside.* I ride for my Lord, the King.' "

Again the knight bowed low and promised to obey the command. A touch of his spurs and the black horse and his rider flew across the drawbridge and down through the valleys and plains. He had hoped to have danger to fight. Deep in his heart he was sorry for the task that had been

assigned to him. But he was a knight, and he was
on service for his king.

Then, even as the King said, there came those
who would ask him to stay. Sometimes the cool of
the evening tempted him to rest after the heat of
the day. Beautiful maidens were all about who
would sing to him, play for him, and help him to
forget his tired body.

Sometimes other knights joined him, and as they
told him of needs all about him, he longed to stay
for only a day and do some deed of valor. But he
was a messenger of the King. He had promised to
obey. Once a deed of shame made him very angry
and he longed to punish the offender.

Once an old man stopped him in the way and
asked to be carried on his horse to a distant town.
Surely he was supposed to do deeds of kindness.
He even stepped from the horse to help him. But
he remembered the command of the King.

"To all these thou shalt say, 'Stand aside. I
ride for my Lord, the King?' "

So again he mounted and went on his way to meet
new and harder temptations..

Finally his errand was done and he turned again
to the castle. His horse, which had been so splendid when he had started, now looked worn and
thin. His armor was dulled from lack of care.
His face looked tired and perplexed. So many
times he had had to do that which he had not
wanted to do. So many times he had had to make
a choice that was hard to make. The quest had
seemed so commonplace when he had started, yet
it had been full of hard things. Why had he been

given such a quest when he could have done brave and valiant things for his Lord?

The old, gray castle drew nearer. He saw the drawbridge let down. He saw some one ride forth to meet him. He heard the sound of trumpets. His horse raised her drooping head and hurried forward. The knight lifted his shoulders and eagerly waited for the messenger.

And lo! It was the King himself. His face shone with happiness as he said,

"Thou hast met the test, oh Knight. Thou hast met the test. To obey was thy command. To obey, when pleasure and fame and love call aside, is a harder task than to fight and to suffer and to die. He that ruleth himself is mightier than he that taketh a city. See, I have brought thee the shield which thou cravest. Take it. Wear it. Then shall all know that thou hast learned the great lesson of obedience. Henceforth thou shalt be called, 'Sir Edward, the Trusty.' "

Gladly Sir Edward laid aside the shield which was dulled and rusty. He lifted to his breast the new shield which the king had brought. Then with humble heart, he saw, written across the top of the shield, the words which he had had to say so many times during the long, hard ride through the kingdom,

"Stand aside! I ride for my Lord, the King."

THE BOY WHO LOST

JACK lived in the slums of one of our cities. As a little fellow he used to go to one of the Sunday Schools in the neighborhood; but most of the boys who lived around his home did not go, and somehow Jack wanted to be like them. So he just stopped going, too. He thought it was not like a real boy to go to Sunday School. He was too big to go.

But after that he seemed to get into trouble very often. Several times he was almost caught when he was in mischief with the other boys with whom he chummed. So his mother took him out of school and had him go to work, thinking that perhaps that would help him to be a better boy.

One day, when he was eighteen years old, he was standing on the street corner with his friends. All were wondering what they should do for amusement when another boy came up and said,

"Fellows, the window is open in the store on the corner and the street light is not lit. Come on and we will have some fun."

The others started to run but Jack called out,

"Hold on fellows. Suppose we get caught in there. We had better not do that."

A great laugh went up from his friends as they called back,

"Listen to the 'goody' boy. You had better go to Sunday School if you are so good. Who's afraid of getting caught?"

He hesitated. Down in his heart he knew he ought not to go. But he didn't want to be laughed at and called a "goody" boy. So he followed after them, climbed in the window, and joined them at the candy counter where they were helping themselves. All were so busy that they did not hear the latch turn. There was a swift movement of some policemen and then six boys were put into the police wagon and taken to the station house.

When Jack's mother heard where he had been taken, she went at once to the mission church and asked them to help her. Gladly they went with her, talked with the Judge, and then promised to help him to be a good boy if the Judge would let him go for this once. And the Judge, wishing to please the minister, paroled the boy on condition that for a whole year he should never once be absent from the Sunday School.

For a few Sundays it was easy to keep his promise. The boys were some of them in jail. Others were not allowed to come to the street corner, so Jack went very faithfully to the class to which he had been assigned.

Now in those months and years which had gone by he had learned not to care for that which was fine and true. So he broke his word and went to the beach, to the game, to the theater.

"The minister will never tell on me. He is a good friend of mine. I am not going to go with those boys. They are too good for me. I like real boys," said Jack to himself.

But the minister had to tell, for he was supposed to report to the Judge at the end of every month. And so it happened that one Sunday a policeman came to the home, dragged Jack out of bed, and took him back to jail.

On the following morning when he was brought before Judge Fawcett for sentence, the Judge looked at him sternly, and said,

"Jack, I have seen your friends who came to plead for you when you were here before. I have found out much about your life during these last three years. You have broken your parole. You have refused to listen to your friends who were trying to help you after you had been such a coward as to leave that which was right for you to do. I find that all attempts to have you go to Sunday School have failed. So I sentence you to the Reformatory for two years.

"In the five years that I have been sitting on this bench, I have had twenty-seven hundred boys before me for trial. Not one of those twenty-seven hundred boys was a regular attendant at Sunday School. Had you continued in Sunday School, I am sure you would not have been before me here. To stick to that which is right is heroic; to leave it is to be a coward. You have chosen the latter way. You are committed to the Reformatory."

So he served his time there, lonely, heartsick, ashamed. And even there, his friends of the School still remembered and loved him. Cards, and fruit, and books made their way to the boy who chose to forget the church and love the street; who chose to think that his best friends were those of the street gang; who chose to do as he pleased. And when he had had time to think about it Jack came to know what real, Christian friendship might mean in his life.

HOW A LIBRARY WAS BUILT

ON the corner of a street stood a newsboy, calling out to all the passers-by that he had the latest edition of the daily papers. It was winter time and the boy was cold and hungry. His face showed lack of love and his clothing showed lack of care.

For two years he had sold papers on that corner. How well he remembered the first day when he had come with his bundle of papers under his arm! His parents had been immigrants and he was a stranger in a strange land, trying to speak a strange tongue. He had been very lonely then. But when the work was over, he could go home and talk over with mother the things which had happened—the thoughtlessness of some of the people, the unkindness of some of the boys, the pleasant word that had come to him from some customer.

But now he was more than lonely. Father had died soon after they had come to America. Then mother had died and at nine years of age he was an orphan and alone. He had a room with the people with whom his father and mother had lived. But he was lonely for friends, for love, and especially for mother. The loneliness showed on his face. Cheerful newsboys secured the trade and he found it hard to make enough to pay for his board. So he was not very happy.

As he stood thinking about it, an old man came

down the street and as he went by the boy, a book, which he had been holding under his arm, dropped to the street. The newsboy did not see it drop, but when he turned to look after the old man who had such a kindly face, the book was lying on the walk. He knew that the man had dropped it, so he ran quickly after him and handed the book to him.

"Well, well! Did I drop that book? Thank you, my boy. That is my library book and I am on my way there. I should have been surprised not to find it when I had reached the library. Have you ever been there for a book?"

"No," said the boy timidly. "I have gone by many times but I have never been inside. It is very big, isn't it?"

"Will you do something for me," asked the man kindly.

"Yes, sir," said the boy. "I shall be glad to do anything for you." It was the first kind word any one had spoken to him since his mother had died and he liked the friendly old man.

"Here is my card. Go up to the library, please. Give this to the woman at the desk and she will check off the book. Look about all you like. When you get ready to go home, give the card to the librarian, tell her what kind of book you would like and she will find it for you. Take a book home with you tonight for your kindness to me."

"I will, sir," said the boy. "Thank you." Then he went back to his work.

But as the hours went by, he became very uneasy about that which he had promised to do. How could he go into that big, strange building? What would they say to him? At last his papers were sold and with heavy footsteps, he turned toward the library. It seemed so big to the shy little boy. Over and over he looked at the card which he was holding fast in his dirty little hand. But he walked more and more slowly as he came nearer to the building. He stopped right in front of it and looked about him. How many, many steps there were to climb! How many people were coming out and going in! More than anything else he just wanted to run away as fast as ever he could go.

But he had promised the man who had been so kind to him. He couldn't break his promise. If he didn't go in, what should he do with the card which belonged to the man? No, he must go in anyway, even though he was afraid.

He pushed the great door open and peeped in. His hands trembled and his heart was beating very fast as he went slowly up the many, many steps which he found inside the door. In one corner was a policeman and the newsboy was very sure that he was going to ask him what he was doing there. So he hurried past him and then followed the crowd until he came to the desk of the librarian.

He gave the book and the card to her and, to his surprise, she said very pleasantly,

"Oh, yes, you are the newsboy who found the book. Mr. Webster telephoned me to be on the look-out for you when you came. What do you like to read about? I should be glad to find your book for you."

Of course all his fear just ran away and he said to her,

"I like mechanics."

Then, together, they went into another room and

she found him a wonderful book, very simple and
very plain for a little fellow to read. Happy as a
prince, he hurried back down the big stairs and out
of the building. He read the book through and
in less than a week he was back for another book,
and then another, and then another. He was no
longer lonely, for he had found friends in his
books.

Soon he knew much about mechanics. He secured a place as a helper to a mechanic. Here he
soon showed how much he could help. Then he
went into a factory as a mechanic there. He was
faithful and he still loved to study, so he rose to
foreman, then to superintendent and finally to man-
ager of the great factory.

By this time he had plenty of money and in his
heart was a desire to help some one as Mr. Webster, the old man who had loaned him his card at
the library, had helped him. He thought about it
for a long time. All that he was he owed to that
first visit to the library. But he still remembered
how big and full of strange things it had seemed to
him as a boy. He remembered how hard it had
been for him to start to enter the place.

"A library should be a place where children love
to go; where there are many things to make them
want to go," said Mr. Vaughn, our newsboy friend.
I will build a library for children and give it to the
city. It shall be very beautiful, but not so big and
grand as the other. It shall have paintings and
pieces of statuary that shall tell the children of the
book-people of the world, and make them want to
read. I will make the children want to go to my
library. Then perhaps I can help some one else as

Mr. Webster helped me when I needed help so much."

So he bought the ground and had a beautiful building made for the children. There were great sunny windows; there were wonderful pictures of the children whom all child-readers have learned to love. There were librarians there who were sunny and friendly, just like the librarian who helped him. There was a great room where the children could gather for stories and games. There was a fountain where the fish could play in the summer time. It was all for the children.

When it was all done and ready for the children to come, Mr. Vaughn gave it to that city in the central part of the United States. It was the first public speech that that newsboy had ever made, so, of course, it was not easy. He told this story which I have told to you and then he said,

"I have tried to make a friendly and homelike library. I shall be satisfied if it means to just one little, lonely stranger what that other library meant to me. I am glad to give it to boys and girls of the city."

NOT WITHOUT GOD

THE streets of the city of Boston were blocked with people, hurrying here and there, making ready for the Christmas season. The street car, pushing its way through the street, was often halted and so John, a boy of seven, had plenty of time to watch the motorman turn off and on the electricity which should make the car go.

His little face was very eager. Father had explained the use of the arm which went above the car into the air and touched the wire above it. He had showed him how the electricity made the wheels go, but never before had he had such a good chance to see the motorman work. He leaned far over the seat, saying nothing but thinking much.

The people in the car were interested in watching him.

"He will be an electrician," said one.

"He has an eager mind," said another.

"I wonder of what he is thinking," said the third. "I should like to know."

Just then the car came to a stop and the motorman who had seen the little face peering at him, said kindly,

"Hello, sonny. Wouldn't you like to drive this car? I'm a pretty smart chap to make this car go and carry you along the street. Don't you think so?"

A smile flitted across the face of the boy as he looked up from the steering gear.

"Yes, I guess you are a pretty smart man all right. But you couldn't make it go one bit without God, could you?"

The motorman was silent. The people in the car were silent. His shrill little voice had pierced to every corner of the car and the people, who had wondered of what he was thinking, were now thinking themselves.

The bell rang and the car started ahead. Finally the motorman turned again to the boy as the car came to another stop and said,

"Thank you, boy. I guess I needed that help that you gave to me. I turn the wheel as I have been taught to do—but God sends the power to make the car go. I couldn't go one bit without His help."

I WILL

THE little, old lumber wagon rolled on, and on, and on, and the girl of twelve on the front seat of the wagon looked in vain for the new home to which they were going. Over the plain, through the lonely, lonely forest, sometimes crossing the swollen rivers they went. None of the persons in the wagon had ever been to this new home and so they were all eager to see it. Father had told them much about it when he had returned from Michigan to Massachusetts and sent the little family on, alone, to live in the house which he had built.

Would she like it? Would there be other girls near the home? Would they be near to the Indians? Would she have time to read the books which were in the box on which she was sitting. These were the questions which came, one after another, to the sweet-faced girl.

One hundred miles from the place where they had left the train; forty miles from the post office; six miles from a neighbor they found the house for which they were looking. And what a house! It was made of logs which the father had hewn from the trees when he had been there. It had no floor but the ground. It had a hole for a window but no glass to cover it. It was bare and cheerless, yet here they must live and make a home for themselves. All about them were forests where the wolves howled and the wildcats prowled. The homes of the Indians were all about them, and Anna wondered if their camp fire would drive away the animals and bring the Indians.

The little family lifted their things from the wagon and looked about them. Then they just lost all the courage which they had had during the long, hard journey. They huddled close together during the long, long night and wondered what was ever to become of them. The mother was an invalid and could not stand unless some one helped her. The boy was only eight so to the girls came the big, big burden in the new home.

But Anna, though only twelve, had a will that knew no such word as failure. After she had looked all about her on the following day, she just gritted her teeth hard and said,

"We are here and we have to stay. I will conquer in the fight."

So, with her sisters, she set to work to make the log cabin livable. They made the floor from trees which they had cut down in the forest. They went the weary miles to a store for the glass and put in the windows to protect them from the cold. They made furniture that they needed to use. They planted the little ground which they owned; they dug a well so that they might have water; and the long hard months went by. Sometimes Anna was a farmer, sometimes a woodsman; sometimes a carpenter. So there was little time to read the books which had come with them from the East. But Anna wanted to learn. She had a bright mind and it was not satisfied only to know all the new things which the hard life had taught her; over and over, she said to herself,

"I will learn. I must learn. Some day I will make a name for myself, somewhere."

At last, to her joy she heard that a school was to open three miles away. There was so much work to be done that it meant getting up very early in the morning in order to finish it before going to school. But Anna wanted to learn, so the first day found her in school. How happy she was as she studied her lessons! But there came a day when the teacher said to her,

"Anna, you know more than I do. I would rather that you did not come to the school for I must give my time to the rest." And the heart of the brave girl just sank. How could she make a name for herself if she could not go to school? She read, and reread the books in the home until she knew them by heart, but still she longed to know more.

When Anna was fourteen years old, her father came from the East but he was little help on the farm. He had brought some new books with him and Anna would read in the books and then go out in the fields to work. All about the farm were many stumps of trees. On one of these the girl would jump. Then she would make believe that the rest of the stumps were people, and she would tell to them what she had been learning.

Little by little, a great desire was growing in her mind. Every time she talked to the trees it grew, until she was sure of the thing that she wanted to be.

"I will be a preacher," she said. "I want to tell to others the story of Jesus. I don't know how it can ever be done but, somehow, I am going to be a preacher. I am sure people will listen to me some day."

At fifteen she was teaching a little school and she hoped, with her two dollars a week, to find some way to go to school; but the war came and father and brother went with the troops, so she had all the work of the home to do again.

Finally a glad day came when she could go to a distant town and enter a school, living with her sister. Eagerly she studied and so she soon took her stand in the school life. The debating team was where she showed her keen mind. Always before her was that determination,

"I will be a minister."

When one can do a thing well, opportunities always come, and soon there came a chance to preach a sermon. At first she was afraid to trust herself. Then she remembered how much it might mean to her so again she just said firmly,

"I know I can and I will."

But her family were not pleased with the idea of her being a minister so they said to her,

"If you will give it up and do something which a woman ought to do, we will send you to college when you have finished the high school. You may have twenty-four hours in which to decide."

College! Her dream could come true. Should she do it?

The next day was an eventful one for Anna for she had one of two ways to choose. And she chose the hard one.

"I thank you for your offer," she said, "but I cannot take it. I will go to college and I will also be a minister."

The days ahead were lonely, for her family were angry with her. But she had some friends who were very kind to her and who were sure that she could make a success of her life.

Soon she was in college, preaching and talking on temperance to help her earn money enough to stay there. Then she knew she needed training in a school for ministers, so she said,

"I will go to Boston. No women are there in the Seminary but I will show them that I can do the work."

She entered Boston University but oh! she was so poor. Her little room on Tremont Street was cold and she had little to eat; but she pushed ahead and she graduated, free of debt, and with a little money in her pocket. Even then she was not satisfied and a few years later she again studied in the Medical School in order to make her life more useful.

At this time a great new work was developing and it needed some one who had learned how to say, "I will," and then to do the thing that needed to be done. By this time people were beginning to know that little Anna who had preached to the stumps so many years before. So they went to her and said,

"We need you to be the head of the work for women. We must win the right of suffrage for them. Will you come?

This would be preaching the gospel of freedom to a world instead of just to a church and gladly she gave her life to the work. Gladly again she said, "I will."

With all her courage and strength she fought for the cause. All over the world she traveled; in every state in the union she told of the need; before many of the great ones of the world she preached temperance and reform through giving women the right to vote. And soon she came to be known as one of the great, great women of the world.

Over and over during her life there had come to her hard places where she had had to say,

"I will. It is the way to success. I just will."

And when the end came in 1919 and Dr. Anna Howard Shaw's work was done, her battles had been won. She had won for herself a good education; she had been a great preacher and a great leader. Temperance and suffrage had been victorious and all the world was ready to say,

"She said she would, and she did."

A KNIGHT OF THE BATH

IN the days of King George of England there
lived a boy who longed to become a knight.
When he saw the Knights of the Bath riding by on
their horses in their beautiful colored garments, he
longed to grow up and perhaps be one of the
knights. As he watched them day by day, he saw
that they were all soldiers; so he decided to be a
soldier also. He found that they had all done some
glorious deed, and so he sought for great things to
do. He was told that they were kindly of heart and
pure in life; so he modeled his life by theirs.

Of course, as the days went by, he grew strong
in purpose and brave of soul. He trained his mind
to think and his body to do that which a knight
would think and do. And soon his bravery and his
goodness came to the ears of the king and the other
knights. "He is worthy to be a knight," they said.
"He has proved that he can be brave and true."

What a happy day it was when the boy, now
grown to young manhood, was told that he would
be allowed to join the brotherhood of the noblest
men in the kingdom! All the day long he was
happy and eager to go to the great church where he
was to be received.

At evening time there came for him a few of the
knights. They placed him in the Prince's chamber
of Westminster Abbey. His hair was cut, his head
was shaved and then he was led into a room hung

135

with rare tapestries where a beautiful tub containing water was in readiness for a bath. Here he was met by one of the wisest and oldest of the knights, who told him of the honor of the order of the bath, of the meaning of the election, and of the desire that he come to it clean of body and clean of soul. He urged him to be known as one who dared great things for the right.

Along the corridor music could be heard, and as the musicians stopped near the door, the knight elect was placed in the bath. Then brave knights, one after another, came quietly to the tub and in low tones told him of the privilege that was his. They bade him keep body and mind undefiled because he was a knight and loved true things. One after another lifted a little of the water and placed it on his shoulders as a sign of brotherhood arfd of common purpose.

After all had gone, he was taken to his couch, bathed in sweet perfumes and dressed in warm clothing. His gown was made of russet red and had sleeves reaching to the ground. Around his waist was a cordon of colored silk. On his head was a russet hood like unto that which the hermit wears. Hanging to his girdle was a white napkin, the sign of purity.

When all was ready and the old church was very still, he was led through the corridors where many great men before him had walked, and then to the chapel of Henry VIII. Minstrels were playing and the knights were there, banqueting to show their happiness that another was to be added to their number. But the knight-elect was allowed no food. He looked about at the chairs of the knights arranged about the sides of the chapel. He saw their crests and their flags. He saw their shields and their helmets above the chairs. Soon he, too, would be entitled to all of these things if only he could hold firmly to his resolve. How proud he was to have been called!

When all had gone from the room for the night except the wisest knight and several attendants, then the young man was led to the altar and given his sword in his hand. Before him burned a holy light and near it was a sacred chalice, a sign of struggle. And here, through the long hours of the night he must kneel, motionless and alone, save for the attendant who at intervals trimmed the light to keep it steady and true.

The night was long and hard. His knees ached from contact with the hard stone floor. He longed for sleep, yet he must remain steady until dawn. He had only his thoughts for company. And his thoughts were all of his great desire to become a Knight of the Bath. So the hours went by and the morning light came. With it came the knights for the morning prayers. How eager they were to see if he had kept his vigil! How gladly they helped him to his feet and gave him time to lie and rest on the carefully prepared bed in the prince's chamber.

Then with music and singing the King came and the knight was brought before him. He had earned the right to hear the call; he had been made ready for the brotherhood; he had kept the vigil through the night. So he knelt before the King and the King bent over him and gladly said as he touched him with his sword, "Arise, Sir Knight and Follower of the King. Your King has dubbed you a Knight of the Bath. You have proved yourself worthy."

Then they put on him the robe of the knight; they made ready the chair against the wall; they pinned on his breast the sign of the order that all the world might know that he had stood the test, had been made a Knight of the Bath and was a follower of the King.

A KNIGHT OF THE CROSS

NOT so long ago, in a place not far from here, there lived a lad who longed to be a knight. When he looked about him he saw many men whom he knew were already knights, and they had a wonderful name—Knights of the Cross—Christian. These men were those whom he loved and admired most of all the men he knew. They were the men who had been kind and loving to him ever since he was a little fellow and he wanted to be like them. So he decided that he wanted to be a Christian knight. Some were doctors and some were merchants and some were men from the farm, but one there was who was wisest and gentlest of them all and whom the lad admired most of all. He was the leader of the knights and knew most about the King, and the knights lovingly called him "Pastor." He it was whom the lad wanted to be like.

He watched the knights from day to day as they went about their work. He found that they had all done great deeds of love and sacrifice for their King; so he sought for great deeds that he might do. He saw that they were kindly of heart and pure of life; so he modeled his life by theirs.

Of course, he grew strong of purpose and brave of soul, for he had true men to copy as he grew. He trained his mind to think good thoughts and his body to do that which a Christian would do. And soon his helpful service and his eager work came to the notice of the King and the other Knights of the Cross.

"He is worthy to belong to our brotherhood," they said. "He has proved that he can be brave and true. Let us make him one of our number."

What a happy day it was for the lad when the word came to him that he would be allowed to join the brotherhood of the Knights of the Cross. All the day he was happy and eager to go to the church and say to the men of the brotherhood that he would be glad to try to serve the King with them. He longed to be a real knight, and this would give him the better chance to serve.

So he watched the gate as the evening came, and with the evening came several of the knights. They took him to the beautiful church which all the knights loved so well. The room in which the knights were met together was hung with beautiful pictures. There was the son of the great King when he, too, was a boy. There was the picture of the army of Christian Knights who had gone forth to fight for the King in other lands. And as the lad looked about the room, he felt that he was to become much more worth while when he was brother to all of these.

When all had come, the wisest of the knights brought the lad to the rest, told of the things which he had seen him do and asked that he be allowed to join the brotherhood, and the knights smiled and held out their hands in welcome to the lad. They told him of the honor of the brotherhood, of the great work which it had done in the world for the King. They told him of the need of strong young knights. They told him of their desire that he should come into the brotherhood clean of body and pure of soul.

And as they talked, the eyes of the lad glowed with living fire. These were his heroes, for he had seen them do great deeds. He would try his best to honor the King and do his work if they would allow him to join the brotherhood.

Then they took him to the altar of the church and he knelt there while the wisest knight laid his hand on his head and prayed that he might be strong and true; that he might go forth to conquer. On his head he placed pure, cold water, a sign of the purity of soul which the boy longed to have. It was to be a pledge of loyalty. It thrilled his very soul. It was the first of the signs that he was to belong to the King and the lad's heart was full of gladness.

As he rose to his feet, he found the other knights also kneeling near to him. And as they rose, they placed their hands on his shoulders and told him of the great work ahead of him. They urged him to keep body and mind undefiled because he was a knight and loved true things.

When they had left him alone at the door of his home, the lad went to his room to keep his vigil, alone with God. Tomorrow all the world should know that he had joined the brotherhood and was waiting for the command of the King. It was to be one of the great days of his life. He thought over the words of the knights and determined that he, too, would some day help another lad as they had helped him. And as he knelt in prayer, he asked the King to come into his life and stay.

When the morning was come, he dressed with care and went gladly to the altar of the church.

There was the beautiful music; there were palms and flowers. There were friends there who had come to see him take the vow of brotherhood. And before them he took the vow of the Christian, promising to go out to fight for the right, to try to keep his life clean and strong, to honor the King.

Then the wisest of the knights, the one whom he loved the most and whom he longed to be like—the one whom the others called Pastor—took him by the hand. There was strength and courage just in the grip of his hand as he said to the boy:

"You have been found worthy to be called to service and to join the brotherhood. You have been made ready to be a faithful follower, for you have been carefully taught in the way. You have taken your vow before all people. So I name you a member of the brotherhood, but only God can give you the sign of the brotherhood. That you must earn from him as the days go by. It shall be seen in your face as it grows stronger and more beautiful. It shall be seen in your hands as they grow more useful. It shall be seen in your life as it grows more like the Christ, the son of the King."

Then the lad went forth with the brotherhood to help him and inspire him. There were many hours of patient waiting; there were days and days of pain and struggle; there were hours when he longed to fly from it all and rest. But always there was the light which had come to him as he knelt in the church. Always there was the brotherhood to help him. Always there was the face of the King before him. And the conquests were won because he was brave and true.

Then lo! as the days went by, he heard the voice of the King in the depths of his soul,

"Arise! Look up, Knight of the Cross and Follower of the King. Your King has watched your vigil and has found you true to your vow. Your King names you a Knight of the Cross—a Christian."

And the world, too, looked into his face, into his eyes, into his life and into his character as the days went by and they, too, called him

"A Christian—A Knight of the Cross."

TRUE-HEARTED, WHOLE-HEARTED

IN the very heart of the beautiful mountains of Switzerland lies the city of Lucerne. The city itself is quaint and attractive; the lake, which shimmers before the city, is blue as the sky above it. The little Swiss chalets on the mountain side seem to beg one to climb and spend the night in their shelter. The mountain peaks, covered with snow and glistening in sunlight and moonlight, seem to touch the very heavens as they go up, and up, and up. The lonely shepherd, climbing with the sheep, knows only too well how steep and how still the sides of the mountain may be. Lucerne is one of God's own beauty spots of the earth.

On a day, not so long ago, ten Christian young men stood in one of the parks of Lucerne looking at a great lion carved in stone in the side of the cliff. The rock of gray sandstone, draped in bits of green vine and gray moss, hemmed in the cavity where the lion lay, as if guarding it from harm. Below in the lake, the scene was mirrored in all its beauty.

The giant figure of the lion seemed to have crawled back into the cave to die, for an arrow had entered his breast and pierced the great heart of the beast. Pain and suffering were written on every line of his face, yet it was not the suffering of the lion which most attracted the attention of the young men standing before the wall of rock.

It was a shield—the shield of France which
rested under the paw of the lion. There were fleur-
de-lis of France and his head had fallen close to
them. No harm should come to them while he had
life.

Below the lion were the names of many, many
men and above the lion were written these words,
Fidei ac Virtuti Helvetiorum. "To the fidelity and
valor of the Helvetii."

"I wish I knew more about it," said one of the
young men.

"May I tell you?" a voice answered. "We, who
live here, love the lion of Lucerne." And they
turned to find a bent old man looking lovingly at
the sculptured lion.

"It was the great Thorwaldsen who gave it to
us here in the rock. Nowhere has he left a finer
piece of work. But nowhere did he have anything
more true and noble about which to work.

"In the days of Louis XVI of France, many of
our men were sent to Paris and became the guard
of the foolish, foolish king and his queen, Marie
Antoinette. You remember the story of the awful
day, August 10, 1792, when the mob stormed Paris
and demanded the life of the king and queen! From
one place to another they fled. Finally they hid in
the Tuileries Palace, and on the steps to guard them
stood our men. Twenty-six officers and nearly eight
hundred men there were, sir; our bravest men, our
fathers and our sons.

"They knew it was of no use; they knew that
they should lose their lives if they withstood the
mob. But they were men of Switzerland—they
were guarding the honor of France. They were

men of honor and so they stood till they fell, cut to pieces for doing that which they knew was their duty to do. See sir, read for yourself. 'To the fidelity and valor of the Helvetii.' Well did Thorwaldsen choose this great lion to represent them. Well did he drive him back and back into the cave, guarding the shield of France. So, today, we honor them. Our children play here. They pat the old lion and they want to be like the heroes, brave and true."

There was quiet in the little party as the old man turned away. There was a feeling of deep appreciation as they looked at the great monument, famous all over the world.

Thoughtfully, the young man spoke again,

"Not a dishonored king do we serve; not a losing battle do we fight; not for a doomed principle are we working. Men, I want to sing. Will you join in the chorus with me?"

Then across the lake, and up the mountains, and into the blue, blue sky above, there rang this song,

> True-hearted, whole-hearted, faithful and loyal,
>   King of our lives, by thy grace we will be;
> Under the standard, exalted and royal,
>   Strong in thy strength we will battle for thee.
>
> True-hearted, whole-hearted, fullest allegiance,
>   Yielding henceforth to our glorious King;
> Valiant endeavor and loving obedience,
>   Freely and joyously now would we bring.

THE CALL TO SERVE

SITTING under a tree which grew before one of
the old, old sanctuaries in the land of the Hebrews sat a woman. Her dress was that of a
prophetess. Her face was strong and true. All
about her were women who carried great bundles
of wood, who climbed the steep hills with the goats
and sheep, whose lives were hard and long. But
this woman lived here near the sanctuary, loved and
honored by the people of the land. In times of
trouble and of doubt, they came to her from north,
and south, and east, and west. She was Deborah,
the prophetess of Israel.

But Deborah's face was troubled. As she looked
to the north, the lines of care deepened in her face.
She was looking toward the great plain of Esdraelon
which stretched across the northern part of her
country. Here lived many, many Canaanites, a
very powerful tribe of people who did not love the
God of Israel; who persecuted those who did love
that God; and who had planted their towns and
cities in such a way that the Israelites dared not even
pass along the old roadways, lest their produce be
taken away, and perhaps their lives be lost. Little
by little the Canaanites had driven them back into
the hill country to live there, separated from their
neighbors and their temples, in their little rude
huts or tents. So the Israelites had made secret
paths by which they could travel and be safe.

Deborah knew all this. She had traveled many of those paths. She knew how hard their life was being made and because she loved her people, she longed to help. But worse than all was the fact that her people were slowly, but surely, losing their faith in the God of Israel. They were beginning to worship Baal and to believe that God no longer cared for His people. And Deborah knew that when this came to pass, the nation would be lost.

So she sat looking to the north, wondering what she could do to help.

"I am only a woman," she said. "If I were a man, I could go out and fight these robbers, these heathen people. But I am only a woman and what can I do to help? There is no leader now whom the people will follow, but we must have one. Long have I looked for him. I think the best to be found is Barak, the chieftain of the north. He has courage and strength. I cannot fight but there are some things which I can do. I can rally the tribes at the call of the Lord. I can inspire Barak to undertake the task. I can by my own bravery help others to be brave. With God's help, I will try to free Israel."

Thus it happened that a few days later a messenger came to Barak in his home in the north of Canaan, saying, "The word of the Lord has come to Deborah, the prophetess, and she would speak to thee. The Lord hath need of thy strength and thy courage."

Wonderingly Barak left his home and traveled to the sanctuary of Deborah. What could God want him to do? The tribes were so poor and scattered that it seemed useless to try to drive out the enemy. Yet even as he stole his way across Esdraelon and over the mountain passes, he was filled with a great desire to free his people.

Deborah was waiting for Barak. Standing there before the sanctuary, she showed to him the land of promise; she reminded him of the need of a leader. Then she said very solemnly,

"Doth not God command thee to take ten thousand men and go to Mount Tabor and free His people? Behold, even now my messengers are going swiftly among the tribes and this is what they are saying to God's chosen people,

" 'Come up to the help of the Lord against the mighty. Come up to the help of the Lord against the mighty, O ye chosen of Jehovah.' Barak, doth not God command thee to go and lead His people?"

Then as Barak stood before the messenger of God and listened to her words, saw her courage and her faith, he, also, longed to help. But he felt his own weakness. If he must try to do this great thing, he must be very sure that it was God's will; that God was going with him. So he answered Deborah,

"If you will go with me, I will go; but if you will not go with me, then I will not go."

"Surely I will go with thee," said Deborah. "Come let us plan for the defeat of the enemy."

Now when the tribes heard the call of the old ram's horn, and heard the messenger say, "Deborah saith unto thee, 'Come up to the help of the Lord against the mighty,' " they knew that again God was to show His power. He had delivered Moses; He had helped Joshua; He could still deliver. So they left their flocks, and herds, and farms, and came to the sanctuary as Deborah had said. They had had no training for battle but they were ready to serve if God needed their help.

To the north moved the line of men, led by Deborah and Barak, singing their songs of faith and courage. Finally they came to a great hill called Mount Tabor. Like an inverted bowl its head rose straight up from the plain. From the hill they could see in all directions and so could tell where the enemy was about to attack. It was an ideal camping ground.

Of course the news was carried to Sisera, the Canaanitish general, that Barak had encamped on Mount Tabor; so he gathered together many men for battle. He had nine hundred chariots of iron and many horsemen. As they crossed the plain their armor glistened in the sun, and the army of Israel trembled as they saw them come.

But Deborah was there to sing to them of the wonderful power of their God; Barak was there to lead them; and they believed that God, also, was there to help them. So they had courage, and faith, and enthusiasm as helpers. And with those helpers any battle is won ahead of time.

Close to the foot of the Mount Tabor ran a little river called the Kishon. It was only a small river, and the army easily crossed it and made ready for battle, right at the foot of the hill. Barak watched their movements closely, and Deborah stood close by to give him faith in the power of God. He had so little with which to fight and they had so much! How could he hope to win?

Suddenly the voice of Deborah rang out over the

hillside, so that not only Barak but also all his men might hear it,

"Arise, O Barak, this is the day in which Jehovah hath delivered Sisera into your hand. Hath not Jehovah gone out before you?"

Then down the sides of Tabor ran the men and threw themselves into the conflict for God and for their country. The battle began and the Canaanites had every hope of success. But across the plain swept a great thunderstorm. The rain fell in torrents. The plain, which had been dry and hard, now became soaked with the water like a swamp. The horses were frightened and plunged about in the mud, throwing their riders and trampling them under foot. The Israelites, believing that the storm was sent by God to help them, fought the harder, and sang their songs of victory. But the enemy, also believing that the God of the Hebrews was punishing them for fighting His people, became panic-stricken and fled for their lives. Some fell into the Kishon which was now a great, swollen river; some became fast in the mud and lost their lives. All was confusion and disorder. Not a Canaanite was left of all that great, glittering army.

When the sun again shone, the great iron chariots of the enemy were sunk in the mud and there was no one to pull them out again. Sisera had fled and been killed in the mountains; Israel was victorious and the power of the enemy was broken forever.

In the Bible there is written a song which the people sang as they returned to the sanctuary to give thanks to God. It is one of the very oldest parts of our Bible. And this is a part of it.

Arise, arise Deborah!
Arise, arise, strike up the song!
Arise, Barak, be strong!
So shall all thine enemies perish, O Jehovah.
But they who love Him shall be as the sun
Rising in its invincible splendor.

And there in the sanctuary Deborah gave thanks that to her had come the desire to send the call, and to inspire such a great leader. Barak gave thanks that to him had come the call to lead his men to victory; and the people all gave thanks that to them had been given a chance to fight again and win again for the God of Israel. So together they sang the old, old Hebrew song.

"Our God is a great God; He is to be feared above all other Gods. I will sing of the praise of Jehovah, God of Israel."

THE FISHER-BOY

A WAY down on Cape Cod in the little town of Wellfleet, there once lived a boy whom the other boys called "Ikey." His father was a fisherman, and ever since Ikey could remember his father had gone out in his little boat to catch the fish and then had sold them in the homes about them. At first, Ikey had just gone with his father for the fun of riding the big waves, of seeing the great fish jump about on the hook, and of talking to his father. But as he grew older, he, too, had a hook and line; he, too, sold fish in the streets of Wellfleet; he, too, became known as a fisher-lad.

Now his people were very poor but they had come from a good family away back in England, and so the boy also wanted to be something more than a fisherman. Wellfleet seemed small to him and at last his father allowed him to go each week to Boston to sell fish there in that great city. With his basket on his arm, he would go up and down Beacon Street and when the people found out that his fish were always fresh, that he gave full weight, that he was always kind and obliging, they became regular customers of the boy. So he could sell all the fish that he could bring with him.

One day when he was passing up the street, he saw a sign in front of a church saying that a noted man was to speak at noon.

"I should like to hear that man speak," said

153

Ikey to himself. I can never hear a man like that in Wellfleet. I think I will go."

So he hurried as fast as ever he could to deliver his fish. And at noontime he slipped into one of the back seats of the church. His clothes smelled fishy and they weren't as good as most of those worn by the people in the church, but Ikey didn't care. He was there to hear what a great man was going to say. So he listened well. Some men would have used words that a fisher-boy might not understand, but this man talked simply and plainly about using one's life. And as the boy listened, he was helped by what the man had said.

After the service was over, the people stayed about, waiting to speak to the man. And the boy watched them. But boys like to speak to great men also—even more than men and women do—and so Ikey stood in his pew for a while. Then he moved up nearer the front. Perhaps he could hear what the man was saying. At last he stood very near to him, and nearly all the people in the church had gone.

Suddenly the man turned about, saw the boy, knew by the look on his face that he was eager to speak to him and so he said, cheerily,

"Good afternoon, my boy. May God bless you. I hope you grow up to be a great and good man."

The boy grasped his hand, and then turned and left the church. But he was a different boy from the one who had entered an hour before. Picking up his basket from the bushes, he went down the streets saying over and over to himself,

"God bless you. I hope you grow up to be a great and good man."

A great man had said it to him. It was a red-letter day in the life of the fisher-boy. Suddenly he had found what he wanted to be. Not just a fisherman but a great and good man.

Soon he had more customers than he could supply with his basket, so he had a fish-stall. Later he had a place in Faneuil Market. All the time he was studying fish. The deep, blue waters about his home became a great school for him. He went to different parts of the country and studied them in other seas.

When the United States wanted to send some one to Europe on a very important errand, Isaac Rich was chosen among all the fish-dealers of the country as the one best fitted to go. So his name became known all over the world.

He was honest and he was wise, so he became rich. But he loved to help others, so he gave much of it away. Many schools counted him as one of their best friends. The business men called him a great man; but the people who knew him best said that he was a good man, also.

Finally he grew old and he knew that he had not long to live. Often he was seen in conference with men who had dreams of days when Boston should have better schools than it had then. So when the end came in 1872, his friends were not surprised at the contents of his will.

He had left money to many things, but the largest amount was left to help to build in Boston a great school where boys and girls, both rich and poor, might have a chance to get an education. The sum which he left was, at that time, the largest that had ever been given by any American for helping to make education within the reach of all people.

So today there are more than seven thousand students studying in Boston University who are given a chance to be "great and good" partly because, long and long ago, a lecturer said to a little fisher-boy,

"God bless you, my boy. I hope you grow up to be a great and good man."

In the College of Liberal Arts of the University there is a large picture of the man who gave so much to found the school. In the cemetery at Mount Auburn there is a plain marble shaft, which the students often seek out, where the fact is mentioned that he was one of the first trustees of the school, which was then only a small, struggling one.

But the greatest memorial of the man, Isaac Rich, is the University itself which today still holds out a Christian helping hand, saying to thousands who have no money, as well as to the many who have,

"God bless you. I hope you grow up to be a great and good American. I will help you on the way."

THE END